Contemporary Western Romance
Standalones
Perfectly Good Nanny
Bridled Heart
Catch the Rain

Tumbling Creek Ranch Novella Series
8 Seconds to Love
Love Me Anyway
The Wrong Cowboy to Love
Collateral Love

Perfectly Good Nanny

Paty Jager

Windtree Press
Corvallis, OR

PERFECTLY GOOD NANNY
Copyright © 2025 Patricia Jager

Contact Information: info@windtreepress.com
Windtree Press
Corvallis, Oregon
Visit us at: https://windtreepress.com

Cover Art by Covers by Karen
https://coversbykaren.com/

Published in the United States of America
1st Edition 2007
2nd Edition 2025
ISBN 978-1-962065-94-8

Dedication

For my "Cattle Baron" and man of my dreams.

One

For the third time in as many seconds, Brock Hughes asked himself why this brunette with haunted, blue eyes and a lopsided grin stood on his threshold. She wasn't much taller than his twelve-year-old daughter and so thin a good gust of wind could blow her away.

"Did you forget I was arriving today?" Her teasing tone bordered on the edge of flirtatiousness. Why was a strange woman standing on his porch, and flirting as though he knew her?

"Hard to forget something I didn't know."

Her eyes flashed with irritation. "I was told to arrive at," she looked at a paper in her hand, "Haven Ranch –" she looked around. "This is Haven Ranch, isn't it?"

Brock nodded. It was his family's ranch.

She glanced back at the paper, "I was to arrive at Haven Ranch on October fifteenth." She twisted the fancy watch on her slim wrist to look at the face. "And it is the fifteenth."

Brock rubbed a hand over his face. He didn't know this woman. And he hadn't been to Halverton drinking since Maddie figured out why he was sick every time he came home. The woman standing on his doorstep was too well dressed and fresh looking to be someone from social services.

"I don't know you from Adam." He looked her over from the expensive, shiny shirt that clung to her breasts, down to the brown slacks hugging her hips. His gaze followed the sharp crease in the slacks down to a pair of sandals dulled from the high desert dust, to the tips of her painted toenails. Her clothes shouted city slicker. And he hadn't been to any city in over twenty years.

Very few people visited out here. It was over a hundred miles from any sizeable town and only a county road of dirt and gravel came close to the driveway. He looked over her shoulder at the storm clouds piling up on the horizon. A small foreign car with a rental plate sat in his driveway, the back end piled with luggage.

"From all those suitcases, you look like you're moving in with someone." He studied her, again. "It isn't us."

"Mr. Hughes, that isn't funny."

How did she know his name when he didn't know hers? "Lady, I don't know you, so how do you know me?"

She cocked her hip and glared at him. "I was hired to be a nanny for your children. Don't tell me you had nothing to do with my being hired. I know you're the only parent."

Her knowledge of his marital status raised the hair on the back of his neck. He didn't like people knowing his business. A wail erupted from inside the house. Brock didn't know which confused him more: the woman knowing his name and family particulars or saying she was hired. He blocked out the high-octave wailing and watched her intently.

"Ma'am, I haven't hired anyone in the last six years." He looked her dead in the face. "Someone gave you misinformation because I didn't hire a nanny."

Her body sagged like an empty grain sack for a brief moment before she caught herself and flipped open a cell phone. She stared at it and sighed heavily. "No reception. May I use your phone to call the agency and see about this mix-up?" She waved her hand to the door. "You better go see what's wrong with Tate."

Brock dropped his hand from the doorjamb. "How do you know my son's name?"

"I told you, I've been hired to care for Maddie and Tate." Placing her hands on her hips, she stared at him. The long, pink, well-manicured nails reminded him of Cindy, his second wife. He'd had a taste of a city woman and he didn't want another one whining about the isolation and broken nails.

How desperate must this woman be to come out to this desolate area of southern Oregon on the word of someone she hadn't met?

The wailing increased in volume and grew closer.

"Daddy, Tate got into the sticker bush out back and won't let—" Maddie stopped when her gaze landed on the woman at their front door. His daughter's glance darted from the woman to him and back again.

Brock secretly smiled as Maddie bit her bottom lip,

a sure sign she knew something.

He took Tate from his daughter. Swinging the small child up into his arms, his heart swelled at the way the boy tucked his head against his shoulder. How such a sweet child could have come from the viper he'd married three years before was beyond him.

"Oh, Tate, you have some nasty scratches. Who won—you or the bush?" the woman asked, stepping closer and tweaking the end of Tate's nose.

Her soft, floral scent drifted up to Brock, causing him to take a step back as a flood of memories tore at his heart. Beth, his one and only love and first wife, had worn that perfume.

White Shoulders.

Memories he'd buried after her death, sent him back to the days of young love, when he and Beth couldn't spend enough time together.

"Daddy, Carina won't hurt Tate, she's a nanny." Maddie slapped a hand over her mouth, her eyes widening.

Maddie's admission pulled him out of his trance and answered his questions. He crouched down next to his daughter, balancing Tate on his knee.

"Is there something you forgot to tell me?" he asked as her young eyes glanced from the woman, Carina, and back to him.

"Rayanne said her aunt found a perfectly good man on the internet, so Willie T and I figured we could find us a perfectly good nanny."

The matter-of-fact statement from his tomboy daughter hit a comic nerve. He burst into laughter. Maddie watched him as though he were a cow crazy from hornworm.

"Um…" Carina broke in. "Maddie," she leaned forward to look his daughter in the face, "who is Willie T?"

At the mention of the meddling, old codger, Brock stopped laughing. "Willie T is an interfering old Klamath Indian who's going to get an earful of what I think about his scheme when we see him."

"He said he'd be here when the nanny arrived to smooth things over." Maddie smiled at the woman. "He didn't figure you'd get here till later this afternoon."

"He didn't, did he?" Brock glanced from his daughter to the woman watching him intently. He wasn't sure what to do. A nanny definitely did not fit in the budget right now, even though it would help him keep Johnson from taking Maddie.

"Go call Willie T and tell him to get over here. Now. If he knows what's good for him." Brock motioned for Maddie to move. She scampered into the house, slamming the screen door behind her.

"This is a school day. Why isn't Maddie in school?" The woman asked.

"Because she's home-schooled, Miss…"

"Ms. Valencia. Carina Valencia." She held out her small, thin hand. He looked at the delicate bones and nearly translucent skin as white as milk. She wouldn't last a week out here. She was too frail and weak to handle the isolation and ranch life. He took her hand, barely applying pressure for fear her bones would break.

"And who looks after Tate? Do you have a housekeeper?"

"No. Maddie looks after Tate a good part of the day, and I look after him the rest."

"How does she get her schoolwork done if she's watching an active eighteen-month-old?" Ms. Valencia cocked her head, giving him the same look as a teacher from his childhood. A shiver skittered up his back.

"We do the best we can."

"Daddy, Willie T is on his way." Maddie rushed out the screen door.

"Do we have to wait for him before moving my things into the house?" Ms. Valencia asked, moving toward the steps.

Damn, she not only looked all citied up like his second wife, she was just as bossy.

"Just because he says he hired you doesn't mean you're staying."

She smiled the crooked grin he'd witnessed when he'd opened the door. "One month of my services has been paid." She took hold of Maddie's hand. "Why don't you help me unload my things from the car?"

He watched the woman and his daughter walk down the stairs and across the sparse patch of grass they called a yard. The woman's presence and unspoken disapproval of the way he raised his children irked him. Maddie had gone to school before his first wife, Beth, a woman full of life and loving, died and the woman he wed three years ago had a baby.

He ran a hand through his hair, remembering the bitter words thrown at him by his second wife, Cindy, as she drove off in his newest pickup. She'd tossed the shreds of their wedding certificate in his face while Tate lay in the bassinet screaming.

He wanted to take the maternal chores off Maddie, but he wouldn't take in another woman and have her rip his family apart. Even if there was a woman who lived close enough to come in every day, there wasn't any money to pay her.

Still holding Tate, he walked out to the car. "If Willie T paid for the first month, he can just get his money back. You might as well leave your bags in the car and head back to wherever you came from."

"Mr. Hughes, I understand your discomfort of having someone show up on your doorstep and say they were hired by you when you didn't hire them." She grasped Maddie's chin, lifting her freckled face up for his inspection. "Your daughter deserves a month's break from taking care of her brother. And I wouldn't doubt having someone around to help out would take some burdens off of you. A month has been paid for, take it, and be thankful."

Brock scanned his daughter's pleading face before making eye contact with Ms. Valencia. The woman knew which buttons to push, he'd give her that.

"I'm not saying one way or the other until I talk with Willie T." He didn't miss the glint of triumph in the woman's eyes before she spun back to pull another piece of luggage out of the backseat of the sporty little car. His eyes roamed over her small backside as the brown pants she wore pulled, accenting her curves.

He'd been celibate since Cindy left. He turned from the enticing sight. So far, women had caused him nothing but heartache, and he wasn't going through that wringer again.

Ms. Valencia emerged from the car. She turned and let out a yell. "Get away from there!"

Brock smiled at their cattle dog sniffing her luggage. The territorial hound started to lift a leg above the smallest suitcase. Brock gave two quick, sharp whistles. Roscoe plopped his bottom down but continued to sniff the suitcase.

"Roscoe's just marking his territory."

"That's not his territory, they're mine." The irritation in her voice made it clear she wasn't used to animals.

"It's his territory if it's sitting in his driveway." She pushed past Brock, picking up two suitcases. He grabbed her arm. "I'll take your bags."

"There's no need for you to carry them all when Maddie and I are standing right here and capable of carrying some as well." She looked down where he held her arm. Brock thrust Tate into her arms and picked up the two largest bags.

Carina motioned for Maddie to pick up the smaller bag and follow. She needed time to regroup. When Brock's hand held her, energy shot through her arm. Steadying her nerves from the onslaught of the man's touch, she hugged Tate against her.

The scent of sour milk and baby lotion made her heart lurch. She snuggled her cheek against his. If her baby had lived, it would be just about this age. She'd give anything to be back in Chicago, holding her child and waiting for her husband to come home.

But she wasn't and never would.

She watched the man climbing the steps to the porch. This was her chance to start fresh and leave the past behind. With this assignment and this family.

A good thing about Brock Hughes; he didn't look anything like her ex-husband. Where Perry was fair, charming, and slender, Brock was dark, secretive, and muscled. For such a big man, his long legs carried his slender hips and broad shoulders gracefully.

When Brock had answered the door earlier, her heart nearly thrummed out of her chest. It was the same way she felt when she first met Perry. The memory pierced her heart. How could their marriage have been formed on electrified passion and withered to dust by one hardship?

One thing she knew; if she ever thought of marrying again it wouldn't be to a man who set her body on fire like Perry. It would be to a stable man who was strong and believed in working things out. And one who didn't want children.

The thought twisted her heart. She loved children, but she couldn't go through losing another.

The thunk of their shoes as they all climbed the wooden steps with their burdens, pulled her from her inner thoughts. Brock stepped to the side, allowing her and Maddie to enter the large, old house. She looked up at him as she maneuvered the case and Tate through the doorway.

Brock's collar-length, black hair with gray at the temples reminded her of a professor from college. All the co-eds had drooled over the man. This man wasn't without male magnetism. In fact, he emitted more than her senses could handle. So why hadn't he found someone to help with the children?

His dossier said he'd been married twice. The nanny service did extensive background checks on their clients, which had made it easier for her to leave the safety of Chicago and head out across the country to such an isolated area. That and Georgie's insistence she should be a nanny. Get away from the strict rules a teacher had to adhere to and give some children the real benefit of her knowledge and love. The thought of helping the same children every day and being a part of a family had drawn her to the idea.

Moving into the entry, the furniture in the front room surprised her. Driving up to the house earlier, she'd realized the clapboard had a history. However, it hadn't prepared her for the inside.

She stopped and absorbed the scene. The room looked straight out of an ad in any nineteenth-century periodical. Worn, colorful, hand-braided rugs dotted the scuffed wood floor. A horsehair upholstered couch and chair with crocheted arm covers faced each other in the small living room while oil lamps sat alongside electric lamps atop square tables with carved legs.

"This furniture is in incredible shape." Carina shifted Tate to run an appreciative hand over a large, intricately carved grandfather clock. Her mother would give half her store to have this sitting in the front window drawing in the solid antique connoisseurs.

"That was carved by my great-great-grandfather for my great-great-grandmother." Maddie tipped her head to the clock and continued toward a hand-carved staircase.

"This house has been in your family for many years then." Carina had always marveled at the tales she heard of people remaining on the land of their forefathers. It made sense of Brock's sensitivity to his privacy. She imagined living out in the boonies watching over what had been passed down to you would make a person that way.

Carina followed the girl up the stairs. She stopped halfway, running her palm over the smooth wood polished by many hands over the years. It wouldn't surprise her to find a chamber pot under the bed along with a pitcher and bowl on a stand in the bedroom.

At the top of the stairs, Maddie stopped. "That's Daddy's room." She pointed to the room directly at the top of the stairs. "Over there is Tate's, and then mine." She pointed to the rooms to the right of the stairway. "This one's the bathroom, and that's the guest room, where you'll be sleeping." She moved alongside the railing around the hole for the stairway, and added, "I hope Willie T can talk Daddy into letting you stay longer."

"I hope so, too. I had to settle a lot of things to come out here and would rather not hurry back anytime soon." Carina smoothed the wayward strands of brown hair escaping the girl's braids. What color of hair would her child have had? Would it have been curly or straight? She shook her head. This was why she left—to put her past behind her. The scattering of freckles across the bridge of Maddie's nose and cheeks added to the child's charm. Her baby wouldn't have had freckles. They weren't prominent in either family.

Stop that. Carina chided herself.

"I hope this room will work." Brock's voice and appearance startled her. Carina dropped her hand from where it rested on Maddie's shoulder.

His arm brushed her breasts when he squeezed passed her through the doorway. The tingling went straight to her toes and flushed her face. She'd never been so quickly affected by a man. Not even Perry.

"The room will be fine," she said, turning her head and inspecting where she would spend the next month. The popcorn stitch bedspread across the four-poster bed had to be older than her mother.

"This house is an antique lover's dream." She

moved about the room and eyed the oak wardrobe in the corner.

"They're all things my relatives acquired over the years."

His disinterest surprised her. How could he live in a house with this much history around and act like it was nothing?

"What's for lunch, Maddie?" he asked, facing his daughter and showing Carina as much attention as he did the furniture.

The girl lowered her head to stare at her feet. "I forgot it was getting to be that time."

"Come on, Maddie. Show me the kitchen, and what you have. We'll figure out something." Carina hooked her arm through Maddie's, pulling her out into the hall and down the stairs.

Unpacking could wait. She was hungry after the long drive.

"Which way to the kitchen?" Carina asked at the bottom of the stairs. The hallway leading to the back of the house had new flooring, but it still reflected the history of the house. Maddie ran ahead into a door on the right.

The wood stove in the corner of the kitchen didn't look out of place in this house, but the propane stove next to it did. Carina sat Tate in the antique, wooden highchair. It had to be the same one his father sat in.

"Do you still use the wood stove?" Carina asked as Maddie dug in the cupboards.

"Not since we got the propane stove. It works even when there's no electricity." Maddie held up a can of tomato soup and grinned. "How about cheese sandwiches with this?"

"Sounds good to me."

Watching Maddie in the kitchen made Carina smile. The girl moved about like a woman who'd cooked for a family for years.

"How long have you been taking care of Tate and your dad?" Carina stirred the soup on the stove and watched Maddie's young face screw up in thought as she placed cheese on the slices of bread.

"Well, Tate's almost two, and Cindy, Daddy's second wife and Tate's mom, left when he was about six months old." She scratched her head. "So over a year."

"How have you kept up with your schoolwork?" Carina found it incredulous that the man hadn't found proper care for both the children in that amount of time.

"I home school. We're so remote we can hook up to the school's system and do class from home. When I run into something I don't know, I just log onto the school and ask a teacher." Maddie shrugged her shoulders.

"It's not the same as being there." How could this man think his bright, young daughter would learn enough by using a computer? Some things could only be learned by hands-on experience. Not to mention the interaction with a teacher and other students.

"You can't talk to a teacher about field trips and science projects."

"No, but Willie T teaches me about all the plants and land formations around here."

"The man who hired me?"

"Yeah." Maddie leaned over and whispered. "I was saying I wished I didn't have to watch Tate all the time, and he said Daddy needed a nanny. So we made one of my school projects looking up nanny services and getting one." She placed her hand on Carina's arm. "You aren't mad, are you?"

Her heart went out to the girl. She wanted a normal childhood. Who could fault her for that?

"No."

Kaboom! Thunder rocked the house as lightning flashed outside the window.

Maddie ran out of the kitchen, shouting, "Daddy, it's here. That storm Willie T and I was tracking."

"Willie T and you were tracking," Carina shouted out the door. Once a teacher, always a teacher. She sighed and wondered what a storm in the middle of nowhere would be like. In the city, a storm meant the miserable downpour of rain and irritable people poking you with umbrellas in the streets, elevators, and buses. During the day the thunder couldn't be heard, but late at night when the traffic stilled, she'd lie in bed and hear the rumble and watch the lightning light up the sky.

Her curiosity got the better of her. Carina left the kitchen, walking through the mud room and out the back door onto the small uncovered porch. A flash of lightning zigzagged across the ground as another one struck from the sky nearly blinding her. The crack and sizzle of energy in the air set her hair prickling. Large drops of rain pelted her.

She stood with her face raised to the dark sky and let the water refresh her hot, tired body. Getting ready for the trip had been long and grueling. Her mother had cried buckets about first losing a granddaughter and now a daughter. Carina loved her mother but needed space. Her mother had smothered her since the miscarriage. As if the woman thought her daughter would be taken from this earth as well, and if she clung to her it wouldn't happen.

Between her mother and co-workers, Carina hadn't felt she could pull her life back together without moving away from the memories. Joining the nanny agency had been the first wise thing her best friend, Georgie, had ever come up with. That was until she got here and discovered the man she was to work for didn't want her.

Carina pushed strands of wet hair off her face as the lightning illuminated the sagebrush-dotted landscape. She smiled. You'd never see a sight like this in Chicago. She held her breath watching nature's artistry.

"Ms. Valencia, are you going to come in out of the rain?" Brock's deep, soothing voice chased away the chills of her rain-soaked clothing.

The screen door creaked open, and she stepped through the doorway. Standing inside the door, she looked down at the puddle around her feet.

"Oh, I'm so sorry." She hurried to the utility sink, grabbed a hand towel, and dropped it on the puddle, sopping the water from the well-worn linoleum. Her wet hair fell into her face. She pushed it back and stopped. Brock's large hand grasped her upper arm, hauling her to her feet.

"Why don't you get into some dry clothes?" His gaze moved from her chest to her eyes with reluctance.

Carina glanced down. Her nipples were vivid peaks against her clinging, wet, silk shirt.

"Good idea." She hurried down the hall and up the staircase to the guest room. Closing the door behind her, she leaned against it.

The heat glistening in his eyes as he told her to change reflected a man who hadn't spent an evening with a woman in a while. The grip on her arm branded her skin. Wiping a hand across her warm face, she quelled any sexual reaction she might have to the man. She needed a place to heal, without any distractions.

Two

Brock met Willie T at the back door. It didn't matter the older man was dripping wet; he crooked his finger for the wily codger to follow and stomped down the hall to the office.

"Hi, Willie T!" Maddie called out. The man responded with a jolly hello back.

Once the office door closed, Brock turned all his pent-up frustrations loose.

"What the hell do you think you're doing hiring me a nanny?" Running a hand across the back of his neck, he stared at the man who'd become a second father to him years ago.

"Maddie is too young to be a mother." Willie T crossed his arms and glared at Brock.

"I know that. But what am I supposed to do? Look what happened the last time I tried to get her a mother." Brock sat on the corner of the desk. Rehashing all his poor decisions, the main one, marrying Cindy, took all the starch out of his fury.

"That's the problem, you thought with the wrong

part of your body." The old man wiggled his eyebrows.

"Damn you! I thought you were my friend. I didn't marry Cindy because I had a hard on, like this whole valley seems to think. I was trying to get a female in this house to take care of Maddie."

"You could have hired an old woman to take care of Maddie and took care of your other problems elsewhere."

"Damn it, you old fart, I didn't have you come here to tell me all my mistakes." Brock had to get this discussion reined in before the man turned the tables on him. Which he'd been known to do. "Where'd you get the balls to hire a nanny for me?"

Brock rubbed the back of his neck. The muscles were tightening. The throb of a bazooka-sized headache pounded at the base of his skull.

"Maddie needs a break from Tate. She needs to be a little girl. It is something a person should not miss out on."

"But you and I both know I can't afford to pay a nanny." He looked at the man standing in front of him wearing faded jeans, a thread-bare flannel shirt, and boots that had been patched more times than the years Maddie had been alive. "And neither can you. How in the world did you come up with the money for a month?"

"I sold two horses."

Brock stared at the man. The sale of his horses fed and clothed himself and his family. "You shouldn't have done that. You need that money for your own family."

"You, Maddie, and Tate are my family as well. And I want to keep you all together." His eyes glazed over and his chin jutted out.

His last words sliced through Brock. Since Cindy walked out a year ago, Maddie's grandfather had tried his darnedest to get custody of Maddie. The cantankerous bastard had sent the social services out as well as stirred the school officials in a dander, making Maddie take all kinds of tests.

A nanny would definitely help with his custody battle against Maxwell Johnson.

"I can see your point. I'll need all the arsenal I can get, if I'm going to beat Maxwell Johnson. But I can't afford to keep her more than the month you paid for." Willie T had set his mind to this, and Brock could see there was no way he could get the man to take back his money. His honor would be hurt.

He pointed a finger at Willie T. "I'll keep her a month. But I'm paying you back as soon as the cattle get sold." When the old man started to protest, Brock held up a hand. "I'll not worry about your family because you were foolish."

Brock had never seen this much anger glinting in Willie T's eyes before. He'd gone and said too much. Cowering inside, but not backing down visibly, Brock steadied himself for the onslaught of Willie T's wrath.

"I have done few foolish things in my lifetime." Willie T uncrossed his arms and stepped forward to place a wide hand on Brock's shoulder. "You, young man, have let emotions sway you in the wrong direction. You cannot keep women away from your family. It is what this family needs. A woman's guidance." Now it was his turn to hold up a hand to keep Brock quiet.

"Tate needs mothering, not a child's care. Maddie

is getting to an age where she needs a woman to question and get answers. You need the peace of mind when you are out with the cattle that everything at home is well." He stepped back. "Let this woman into your lives for this month and see if you all don't absorb inner peace."

A knock on the door interrupted their locked gaze. Deep down Brock knew this man spoke what had been weighing on his mind for some time. But why couldn't Ms. Valencia have been some shriveled up old maid?

"Yes," Brock said, glancing at the door as the woman they talked about entered.

"Maddie said Willie T was here, and I wanted to meet him." She glanced briefly at Brock before her eyes lit up and a welcoming smile was bestowed on the man next to him. Brock wondered if the two had met before. The smile on Willie T's lips and the brightness of his eyes were his usual greeting for Maddie.

"Ms. Valencia, it is a pleasure." Willie T clasped her small hand between his wide paws.

"Willie T. That is an interesting name."

"It's short for William Thunder."

Brock cleared his throat. "Is lunch ready?" he asked. The old man's avid attention to the nanny stuck in his craw.

"Yes, that was the other reason I came to get you." She smiled at Willie T and pivoted to exit the room.

Brock took a step toward the door to follow. Willie T grabbed his arm, stopping him. "You need to do whatever you can to keep that woman."

The words hit him like a ten-pound sledge hammer. "Why?"

"She's a keeper."

Shaking his head, trying to make sense of the old man, Brock looked him in the eyes. "What do you mean a keeper?"

"She needs this family as much as you need her."

The man was full of predictions and prophesies. Brock didn't know why he listened to half of what Willie T said.

"We'll see about that," was the only comeback he could think of as he hurried down the hall to eat his mid-day meal and head out to check on the cattle.

Carina found Willie T to be a charming gentleman with a great sense of humor and full of knowledge of the land and people. As she, Maddie, and Willie T discussed the area and people, she noticed Brock gradually pulling out of the conversation. By the time the meal finished, he'd already excused himself without even giving her any clue as to what he expected of her.

"Maddie, where did your father go?" she asked as they cleaned up the kitchen while Willie T entertained Tate in the living room.

"He always heads out in the afternoon to check the cows. He'll be back by dinner time." Her matter-of-fact answer did little to diffuse the irritation building toward this man. She found it unconscionable to leave a twelve-year-old in charge of a toddler for that length of time.

"He'll be gone for hours? What would you do if something happened?" When the child turned troubled eyes on her, Carina knew her anger had shown in her words.

"Daddy or Jack, his helper, check up on us throughout the afternoon, and I know how to use the radio." The girl's words were punctuated with vindication.

"I wasn't trying to say your father is bad. I just need to understand how things work around here."

The smile returned to Maddie's face.

She was forgiven. "Show me the rest of the house and fill me in on the routine."

Maddie chattered like a monkey as they toured the house. Back at the living room, she took Tate from Willie T, swinging the toddler onto her hip like a seasoned mother.

"Ms. Valencia, it was a pleasure to meet you. We'll be seeing one another again soon." Willie T bowed, patted Maddie's cheek, and disappeared down the back hall.

"It's time for Tate's nap," Maddie said, drawing Carina's attention back to the room and from her ponderings about the man. "While he's sleeping you can unpack, and I'll work on my school work."

"Here let me take Tate up to bed since I'm headed that way anyway." Carina took the boy from his sister. He was heavy for his age. How did Maddie lift him like he didn't weigh a thing? "When I get my things put away, I'd like to see what you're working on for school."

Maddie's eyes lit up. "I'm writing a story about the history of our family and working on some tough math problems."

"I'll be down as fast as I can to see if I can help."

Maddie threw her arms around Carina's waist. "I'm happy you're here."

"Me, too." Carina smoothed the girl's unruly hair and smiled into her freckled face. Helping these children was exactly what she needed to take her mind off the past.

***

Brock sat on the front porch after dinner watching the rain pummel the dry earth. Sipping a beer, he scratched Roscoe between the ears. They needed a good rain. The grass was getting scarce. If it didn't last at least one more month, he'd have to start feeding hay sooner than he could afford.

Maddie's giggles, followed by a sultry woman's chuckle, drifted out through the open door. Roscoe perked his ears as Brock's stomach bunched. He couldn't remember the last time a woman's laugh echoed in these walls.

Cindy had been an eyeful, but her tongue and attitude were detrimental to both he and Maddie. It was actually a blessing she'd left. Tate was an intelligent, good-looking, little boy who would grow up in a positive environment. His heart warmed thinking of Tate, the only good thing to come from his second marriage.

Looking back, he hadn't loved Cindy. She'd been on the prowl for a man to take care of her, and he'd been searching for someone to care for Maddie. He snorted. Only it had ended up the other way around. His daughter had waited on Cindy. Just like the mean stepmother in Cinderella.

He kicked the railing in front of him. Roscoe glanced up with sympathetic eyes.

"Yeah, boy, that second time was a big mistake. One I'm not going to make again." He took another gulp of beer. It would be a long time before he let another woman rule his household. The whole incident reinforced his theory he'd never love another woman

29

like he had Beth.

The screen door squeaked, and Maddie stuck her head out. "Daddy, I'm going to bed now. Carina is putting Tate down."

The freckled face and dark braids tugged at his heart. She and Tate were all he needed.

"Come here. You haven't given me a hug today." He set the bottle on the porch next to his chair and opened his arms wide.

Maddie giggled, ran out the door, letting it slam shut behind her, and jumped onto his lap. He hugged her tight and breathed in the scent of his daughter. Horse, cooking, and a faint baby powder scent from taking care of Tate. His heart squeezed.

All the scents he associated with her mother their last years together. The ache he thought had finally faded came back to him with overwhelming clarity.

Maddie hugged him tight around the neck then leaned back. Peering into his eyes, she asked, "Daddy, can we keep Carina longer than a month? Please, she's lots of fun and knows lots of stuff. And she was a teacher before she became a nanny. She could help me with my school work." She batted her long dark lashes and smiled. It reminded him of the seductive smile her mother used on him when she wanted something.

Growling, he pulled her to his heart. He loved his children and wanted to do whatever it took to keep them happy, healthy, and together. Unfortunately, they all had to make some sacrifices right now. If he couldn't keep all his cows and the calves they were birthing alive, there was a good chance of losing the ranch. This was the year he had to pay off the loan against his property. The medical bills from Beth's accident had nearly cost them their home. And if he couldn't keep the ranch, he knew good-n-well Maxwell Johnson would swoop down with all his money and take away Maddie.

The generous offer from his friend at the bank was all that kept his feet on this land. He knew several doctors and lawyers who would love to make his spread into a hobby ranch. The thought of selling his family's legacy to one of them had never crossed his mind.

He'd work from sun up to sun down to keep this place. Just as his father and grandfather before him. And not spend a penny more than necessary. A nanny wasn't necessary. Not as long as he could prove he was a good father.

"Honey, I hate the burdens I've put on you, but right now, even if I wanted a nanny, I couldn't pay her. We don't have the extra money to pay someone to take care of Tate. That's why, unfortunately, it's fallen to you." He hugged her tight, wishing he could give her what she asked for.

"I would give anything for your mother to still be with us, and you to go to school like all your friends." His heart ached for his daughter's plight and the renewed loss he felt for a wife who was ripped from him so early in their marriage. His voice cracked as he added, "I'm sorry, we just can't afford it."

"It's okay, Daddy. I understand." She kissed his cheek and crawled off his lap. Her slow steps reflected her sorrow over the outcome of the conversation.

Damn. He hated the fact he had no skills other than raising cattle and killing people. He rubbed a hand across his face and took another long drink of beer. If he'd had an inclination for anything other than ranching, he'd have left long ago. He tried to learn another trade in the military, his shooting prowess landed him the military profession of a sniper. Can't earn a legal, profitable living off that skill. He took another swig of beer to dull the memories he'd locked away when he returned from the Gulf.

Ranch life was hard. Heartbreaking. And he couldn't think of anything else that filled him with such satisfaction.

"The children are all in bed," Carina said from inside the screen door.

"Thank you." Brock didn't look up. He knew what she wore. After getting soaked in the rain earlier and showing off her womanly attributes, she'd donned a baggy sweatshirt and sweatpants, hiding every one of the luscious curves he'd already witnessed.

"Mind if I join you?" she asked softly.

"No." Where did that come from? He did mind if she joined him. He didn't want to get to know her. If he kept her at a distance for the month, she would remain a stranger, and he wouldn't wonder if Willie T's idea had been a good one.

The screen door opened and slapped shut. Her soft steps scuffed across the boards to the chair beside him. Roscoe stood up, stretched, and wiggle-walked across the porch to the woman.

"I'm sorry to have shown up like this. It had to be a shock. Me standing on your doorstep, saying you hired me. I had no idea it wasn't you. The agency just handed me my assignment." She smiled, letting the dog sniff the back of her hand. "You have one smart daughter. She and Willie T had to give specific information about you so a background check could be done."

"She and her very capable accomplice are quite crafty. It almost worries me the days Willie T spends with her. I never know if I'll find a teepee set up in the corral or the horses painted for war." Brock should have known the two were up to something. Willie T had spent more time at the ranch than usual. "Maddie knows everything about me and the ranch. I'm sure it wasn't hard for her to find whatever they needed."

"It also makes me wonder at how much time she is left alone with just Tate." The woman's eyebrow lifted. "Don't you worry being so far from anywhere about the hours they spend alone?"

"Jack or I check in on them every hour. And she knows how to work the radio. This place is big, but we figure out our schedule each day and make sure one of us can keep an eye on things here." He snickered. "And then there's Willie T. He shows up at all different times and stays usually past a meal." He looked at her concerned face. "They aren't alone as much as you, my ex-father-in-law, or those old biddies at the PTA think."

"I wondered if the school system monitored Maddie." She scooted forward still petting Roscoe. "There's been some great curriculum put together for home school students. Ask the principal at your local school about it."

"How do you know so much about all of this?" Now it was her turn to sit back and search for answers. She watched him for a minute before crossing her arms.

"I forgot you don't know anything about me."

"And you know everything about me," he said with displeasure. She smiled and a glint of mischief twinkled in her blue eyes.

"That bothers you."

"Yes, it bothers me. There's a reason I live two hours from the nearest town and have lots of land around me. I like my privacy."

Carina couldn't help but grin even more. She knew from the minute he leaned against the doorjamb, not allowing her over his threshold, he was a man who kept secrets.

A man with secrets tugged at her curiosity. That was one of the things that kept her on his porch when she'd realized he didn't have a clue who she was.

Taking a deep breath, she recited her decision to become a nanny. "I love teaching. But after a personal crisis, I needed to get away from my past and move forward. Taking a job away from family, friends, and all the memories seemed like a logical choice." She smiled, but her stomach squeezed as his eyes studied her. Those brown eyes probed. Could he see she ran from guilt? Panic squeezed her chest. Carina inhaled a long deep breath. He didn't know anything about her. Not even where she came from since he wasn't the one who hired her.

"How come someone your age isn't married with kids of your own?" He tipped the bottle to his lips and observed her as he swallowed.

Remorse shook her body. She was married, until the miscarriage. How much did she want to tell this man? One she would never meet again after this month.

She cleared her throat. "I was married. But…" she gulped back the humiliation and anger, "my husband divorced me a year ago."

"He divorced you. Why?" His eyes narrowed. The rain pelting the roof grew in volume.

"Not for any reason you have to fear for your

family." She stated. She couldn't tell him the reason, failure to bring their child into the world.

"Because of the divorce you just picked up and ran away?" His accusation hacked away at her little bit of control.

"No. It wasn't just the divorce. There were other circumstances surrounding the divorce that, well, I needed to move on."

The dog put his head in her lap as if sensing her turmoil.

The animal's warmth and acceptance staved off the anxiety of the conversation. She'd always wanted a pet, but living in an apartment over an antique shop, she hadn't been allowed anything other than a goldfish.

"I-I, my medical problems seemed to push us farther apart. Until one day, he decided his work was more important than our marriage." That was all this man needed to know.

Placing her hand on the dog's head, she moved her palm over the smooth, roundness. The warmth under her hand and the sigh from the animal sent a shimmer of excitement through her. This was her one chance to learn about animals firsthand. If the man sitting across from her allowed her to stay.

He leaned forward. "Will your medical problems cause trouble this far from medical facilities?"

Carina jerked her head up and peered into his eyes. She'd only known this man for half a day, and he showed more concern for her welfare than she'd ever witnessed in her husband's eyes.

"No, my health is much improved." Now she felt like a dolt for not telling him the truth.

He nodded toward the dog. "Roscoe likes you. He

doesn't usually take to women."

"He must be a good judge of character," she teased. When Brock didn't respond she glanced over.

He sat back in his chair and stared out into the dark night watching the rain fall from the sky in buckets. Petting the dog, she watched the man. He fought demons. It was clear every time lightning lit up the sky, revealing tortured features etched on his face. The children seemed unaffected. What was the father's torment?

"Does it always rain this hard?" she asked when the silence seemed to choke her.

"Several times a year. We need the rain. The grass needs to last a couple more months."

"Why?" She'd never heard of needing grass to last. Her curiosity over everything was one of the reasons she liked to teach. When teaching you also learn new things.

"I don't have enough hay to feed more than six months. If I have to start feeding the livestock too soon, I won't have enough to keep them fed until the spring grass comes on." He raised the beer bottle to his lips, frowned, looked down the opening, and set the empty bottle on the porch next to his chair.

"Can't you buy more hay?"

He turned dark, angry eyes on her. "No, I can't buy more hay. I can't afford to call the vet if a cow gets sick, and I can't afford to lose one damn calf." He looked her square in the face. His eyes burned with an intensity she'd not witnessed before. Fear crept up her back as the man sprang to his feet.

"And I can't afford a nanny this family needs." He shoved the chair back, yanked open the screen door, and stalked into the house.

Carina sat in the rocking chair, clutching the arms, and wishing the agency had handed her a different assignment. The man of the house was broke and broken. The children were in desperate need of schooling and a woman's touch. But could she endure the man's outbursts even for a month? Perry had never flown into fits of rage. Not even after she lost the baby. He just stared at her and walked away.

The sound of chimes from the grandfather clock in the hallway reminded her she hadn't called Georgie to let her friend know she'd arrived. Carina pushed out of the chair. Wind hurled rain onto the porch splashing her for the second time that day. For being touted the high desert there was sure a lot of moisture in the air.

She closed the screen door carefully, not allowing the door to slam. The lightning flashed, and she saw the dog sitting on the porch.

"Do you come in at night?" she asked, opening the screen. The dog looked at her then turned and walked to the end of the porch.

"Guess not." She closed the screen and the wooden door. Out of habit, she reached up to throw the deadbolt, but there wasn't one. All that kept the world out was a hook that slipped over a nail. Carina rolled her eyes and slowly climbed the stairs in the dark.

In her bedroom, she pulled her cell phone out of her purse and flipped it open. *Shoot, that's right. There wasn't any service out here in the boonies.*

Listening, she caught the sound of someone moving down the hall. He wasn't in bed yet. Did she dare knock and ask to use the phone? If he was so strapped, he might not allow long-distance calls. She chewed on her bottom lip, trying to decide what to do.

She had to call. Georgie had to be going nuts wondering why she hadn't contacted her yet. She could just use the phone and leave him money for the call.

No. She should ask first, it would be what she'd want a guest in her home to do. Taking a deep breath, she squared her shoulders and walked down the hall. Carina knocked on the door and waited.

When there wasn't a reply, she knocked a little louder.

"Maddie, since when…" The door opened, and Brock Hughes stood in front of her in nothing but his tightie whities. She couldn't stop herself from scanning the length of him. Her mouth went dry; regions to the south became wet.

"What do you want?" he asked, crossing his muscular arms and taking the stance of someone defending his property.

"I-I. My cell phone doesn't work."

"I know." He tipped his head in a move that said, 'tell me something I don't know'.

"I need to call a friend and let her know I arrived." She looked at his square jaw and dark eyes. The heat building in his eyes told her the rudeness was to keep her at a distance. And that was exactly what she intended. To stay away from this man and the need he flared in her.

"The phone's in the kitchen."

"I'll pay for the call."

"Not necessary." He dropped his hands to his side. Her gaze followed the motion, darting to the ridge in his briefs. Realizing where she stared, she glanced up. His bulging pecs loomed straight across from her face.

One step and she could kiss the suntanned skin sprinkled with dark, curly hair.

Heat and anger flamed her face. How could a man make emotions rage so strong just by his presence? Not only did his firm, tan body set her core on fire, but his warm voice, dark eyes, and nurturing tugged at her heart.

"I'll pay for the call." She made an about-face and stalked down the stairs to the kitchen.

Carina left the light off and watched the faint flashes of lightning in the distance. Georgie would hear the unease in her voice. She had to calm down before she dialed. Carina crossed the room to the phone hanging on the wall. Breathing in and out like her yoga instructor taught her, she slowly calmed her body.

Punching in the numbers, she hoped Georgie was home and not out partying.

"Hello? This better be Carina, or I'm going to scream."

"Hello, to you."

"Where have you been?" The desperation in her friend's voice added more guilt. Georgie was the only person who knew all her reasons for this job. Her mother still reeled from the news her only child had left the city.

"I'm in Boondocks, U.S.A. and there's no cell phone service."

"Is that really a name of a town?"

"No. I'm at the ranch."

"What's the family like?"

Dark eyes filled with desire and bulging briefs flashed through her senses. She shook her head and cleared her throat. "The daughter is a freckle-faced, blue-eyed, intelligent girl. The boy is adorable." She hoped the longing aching in her heart for her lost child didn't reflect in her words.

"And the father? What's he like?" Carina didn't miss the matchmaking tone in her friend's voice. Georgie had tried setting her up a month after the divorce.

"A bear who woke up too early after hibernating."

Georgie laughed. "No. Really."

"He's a broken man who wants more than he can provide for his children." Carina's heart thudded in her chest. The man's paternal tendencies endeared him to her. Even as she wanted to run from the strong attraction.

"He can't afford a nanny. A friend of the family actually hired me for a month."

"No way. You need more than a month away." She could hear Georgie drumming her fingernails on the phone stand. "Tell him you'll do it for free."

Lightning flashed in the kitchen. A loud 'CRACK' ripped through the house and the line went dead.

Three

She tapped the button several times. Nothing.

"Great!" Carina replaced the receiver and hugged her arms tight around her body. The kitchen grew cold and uninviting. She wished to be back in her big, snuggly bed in Chicago. But she couldn't. There the memories and what-ifs plagued her the worst. They always came in the dark of night. Echoing through her mind, blaming her, working through what she did wrong the day she lost her baby.

Tate let out a wail. Small feet ran down the hall followed by heavy steps. A door closed. She walked up the stairs and down the hall to her room. Crawling under the covers, she listened to the tapping of rain on the window and the deep drone of someone telling a story in Tate's room. Her heart squeezed. Her baby would never hear a story read with a loving voice.

***

In the morning, Carina dressed and headed to the kitchen to make breakfast. The sound of a motor grew louder as she entered the room. The smell of brewing coffee perked her senses. Maddie stood near the sink scrambling eggs.

"You're up early," Carina said, taking the bowl from the girl.

"I always get up and make breakfast for Daddy when he comes in from checking the cows."

"Is the sound I hear his pickup?"

Maddie laughed. "No, that's the generator. The power lines must be down."

"Oh!" Carina listened. The monotone sound of the motor droned at a steady pace. She smiled. "Well, now that we have that straight, how about we spice up these eggs with some onion and bacon?"

Maddie ran to the pantry and pulled out an onion, then to the refrigerator and pulled out a package of bacon. The bacon crackled on the stove when a pickup slid to a stop just short of the back door.

Brock dressed in a warm coat and a cowboy hat sprinted up to the door, shouting, "Maddie, get your boots and coat."

The girl jumped into action without hesitation.

"What's going on?" Carina asked, spinning from the spattering bacon.

"Got a cow down. I need Maddie to drive the pickup."

"She's too young to drive."

"She's been driving since she could reach the pedals. Hurry!" he shouted down the hall as he poured a cup of coffee.

"I'll get Tate. We'll come, too." Carina turned the burners off under the pans.

"You'll just get in the way." The look he threw her told her he didn't want her interfering.

"You can't tell me the help of another adult isn't necessary to get a cow…whatever." She ran upstairs, grabbed a coat, and scooped Tate out of his bed, picking up his shoes and a coat on the way out.

Brock and Maddie trotted to the pickup. Roscoe stood in the back of the vehicle barking, instructing everyone to hurry. Carina slapped the screen door shut behind her and ran to catch up. Tate laughed and patted her head as she ran.

"Scoot," she said, pushing Maddie to the middle of the seat as she and Tate climbed in.

"I told you to stay." Brock glared at her and ground the pickup into gear.

"I said you could use more help." Carina glared back and slammed the door shut. The vehicle spun out of the yard and down the drive. She shoved Tate's feet into his shoes and his arms into the coat.

"Don't you at least have a car seat for Tate?" Carina searched the interior of the cab and spotted an antiquated car seat strapped to the jump seat as Brock jerked his thumb over his shoulder. She leaned over the seat, buckling Tate in as he squealed in delight.

"What do you mean by cow down?" Carina held tight to Tate. The backend end of the pickup swerved one way and then another.

"If a cow lays, say in a hole or small ditch, she can't get up. The more she thrashes about the more she ends up on her back. The gases in her stomachs—"

"Stomachs?" No wonder cows were so big if they had more than one stomach.

"Yeah, stomachs as in three. Anyway, the gases flow and mix causing her to bloat. If she's down too long she actually poisons herself."

Carina's stomach started to gurgle with displeasure. "So, what do you do?"

"Save the cow."

The pickup bounced and slid down the muddy road. The wipers moved sluggishly pushing at the mud thrown up on the windshield by the large tires.

"Eeeee!" Carina shrieked as the pickup slid sideways down the road.

"You should have stayed." Brock gave her an 'I told you so' look as he managed to control the vehicle.

Wiping a hand across her clammy brow, Carina lurched forward when the pickup slid to a stop.

"Now what?" she asked, peering through the mud-streaked windshield. How could he know where he was going? She couldn't see a thing.

"You'll see." He swerved the pickup off the road and over a metal contraption, rattling her teeth. As she tried to ask what that was, they launched over a bump in the road.

A dog yelped.

Tate squealed and laughed, having a great time.

"I see her!" Maddie hollered and pointed.

Brock slammed on the brakes and was out the door followed by Maddie before Carina had time to find the door latch and step out carrying Tate.

Roscoe ran around the mound in the mud, barking.

"Quiet, Roscoe!" Brock ordered before turning to her. "Why'd you take him out of the car seat?" He threw her a disapproving look and returned his attention to the cow. "Stick Tate in the pickup bed and grab that rope."

"But he'll fall out!" Carina stared after the man striding toward the mound in the mud where the dog bounced. He knelt beside a behemoth of an animal and patted its head. Brock talked to the cow in a soothing voice that would have melted her knees if she wasn't so upset with him and the whole episode.

"Put the boy in the bed and bring me the rope!" he ordered, glancing up from the cow.

Did that come from the same man who moments before crooned to the beast?

She glared at Brock's back. Against her better judgment, she placed Tate in the pickup bed and grabbed the coil of rope. She moved toward the cow, Brock, and Maddie. The creature raised its head, a long tongue stretched out of the cow's huge mouth as the animal bawled and rolled her eyes.

Brock grabbed the rope from Carina's hands. He quickly tied a knot around the cow's two front feet. "Maddie get in the pickup. When I yell, go forward slowly."

Carina stared at the man as he looped the other end of the rope on the back of the pickup. What was he thinking?

"Maddie's only twelve. I'll drive." She headed toward the driver's door of the pickup. Tate laughed and slapped the side with his hand. "And Tate's in the back."

Brock moved so fast, she was held tight against him before she knew what happened. "They've both done this before. Maddie, go."

The girl climbed into the driver's seat. The lights in the back end of the pickup flashed red and white as she put it in gear.

When the rope tightened on the cow's leg, Carina realized what they planned. "No! You can't pull on the poor animal's ankle like that." She shoved out of Brock's hold and ran to the hitch, trying to untie the rope.

"It's a hock and it's no different than me pulling a little on your arm." He grabbed her arm and gave a tug, pulling her against him.

Ignoring the sparks of irritation in his eyes, she said, "You aren't as strong as a truck."

"And you don't weigh close to twelve hundred pounds." He pulled her to the side of the vehicle and waved to Maddie. The tires spun, throwing mud up before the pickup slowly pulled the huge animal out of the indention in the ground.

Annoyance at the man's arrogance and her own lack of knowledge infuriated her. A twelve-year-old shouldn't be driving such a large vehicle and definitely not with her baby brother in the back. And then to yank on the animal as if it were an inanimate object. The whole episode seemed barbaric.

"How do you know it doesn't hurt the cow?" she asked not even trying to hide her annoyance.

"I didn't say it didn't hurt. But I'm sure you would rather have a little pain than death."

Carina flinched. She would give anything to be in physical pain and still have her child alive. The emotional agony was hell. His gaze lingered, staring into her eyes. He mustn't see her guilt. If he knew she wasn't capable of keeping her own child alive, how would he react to her taking care of his children?

She motioned to the cow. "How far do you need to pull her?"

"Whoa!" he hollered, and Maddie stopped the vehicle. Brock walked over to the cow. Maddie backed the pickup and Brock removed the rope from the cow's feet. He twisted and looped the rope, sliding it over the beast's head. It resembled the rope contraptions she'd witnessed on horse's heads in magazines.

Brock stood up, still holding the end of the rope. "You two get behind and push. We have to get her in at least a sitting position or we'll lose her."

Maddie hopped out of the pickup cab, up into the back end, and tossed out a pole as long as she was.

"Come on, Carina." The girl grabbed the pole, dragging it to the side opposite of where Brock pulled on the rope and the cow's head.

Carina followed Maddie, who dropped the pole down beside the cow and gave it a kick tight against the animal's back.

"Come on, push," she ordered, pushing on the side of the cow as Brock pulled. Carina touched the rough hair and wrinkled her nose at the smell of cow manure, mud, and the gases slowly seeping out of the animal.

"Push!" Brock hollered and tugged. Carina leaned into the beast and pushed with her legs. The cow moved slightly, and Maddie kicked the pole under the animal, moving her closer and closer to a sitting position. Carina's legs burned from the activity. This was a lot different than running on an inside track three times a week. Her thigh muscles bunched, and her calves seared from the stretching. Satisfaction had crept onto Brock's face, a sign they had the animal just about where he wanted her.

The beast grunted and thrashed with her head and legs.

Maddie fell backward onto her bottom. The animal swung her massive head, butting Brock and knocking him to the ground. He landed with an "oomph". Carina slid into the mud beside the cow. Using the beast to pull herself up, she looked over the mound.

"Are you alright?" she called out. Maddie gave her a weak smile, but Brock didn't move. Fear crept up her spine. She had no clue where to go for help if he was injured. Carina ran to Brock and knelt beside him. The sound of his teeth gritting moments before he opened his eyes chased away her fear.

He shoved her out of the way and headed back to the cow. "Got to get her up, she's been down at least two hours. Who knows how long before I spotted her." He pulled on the rope, again, and Maddie pushed on the beast's side, kicking the pole.

Carina couldn't believe they went back to wallowing in the mud when the animal didn't want any help. Let the thing die.

"Why are you busting yourselves to keep her alive? It's obvious she doesn't want our help." She looked at their mud-covered clothes. "One of us could get hurt. Is it worth that chance?"

"She's worth a thousand dollars and the calf inside of her is worth that much in six months." Brock glared at her. "Push!"

Carina bent down, shoving on the cow, putting all her frustration and anger into moving the animal. He was no different than Perry. He cared more about the money than his family's safety. The knowledge he was no better than the man who left her when she was financially strapped and emotionally empty fueled her efforts. She left a selfish oaf behind only to be up to her knees in mud, pushing on a smelly, stupid cow for another one. Carina looked at the mud-covered man tugging on the rope. His jaw had a determined set as his whole body wrenched on the rope pulling the cow's head.

"She's up. Maddie, curl her legs under her," Brock said between puffs and grunts, pulling on the animal.

Carina kicked the pole under the cow while Maddie tended to the legs.

When the beast sat up in a comfortable position, Brock released the rope and took off his hat, knocking the mud from it. He wiped the sweat from his forehead. Maddie leaned against him, and he gave her a big hug. "Don't know what I'd do without you, Freckles."

Watching the camaraderie and closeness of the two, regret washed through Carina. She'd never know what it felt like to accomplish something with her child. She'd lost her chance to experience that closeness.

She turned from the sight. Sadness and grief enveloped her.

Brock watched the woman before she turned. She was covered with mud. Her hair hung in hanks like a cow's tail. She'd proven she wasn't as fragile as she looked. He smiled and started to comment on her appearance when he noticed the sadness in her eyes. He didn't understand his need to make her smile. But the agony in her eyes tugged at his conscience.

"Not bad for a wisp of a city girl," he said, slapping her on the back with his hat.

"Do you do this often? I never knew cows were so stupid." She kept her eyes cast down at the cow. What was in their depths she tried to hide?

"It mainly happens when there's lots of mud and they're pregnant. They can't get traction to get up, and their bodies are heavier." He looked at her mud-covered clothes. "You'll have to wash those right away. This clay stains the heck out of things."

"Will she be all right?" Carina continued to stare at the cow. "When is she due?"

"We start calving next month. I don't think this caused too much trauma. Cows are pretty tough."

"But this episode could cause her to go into labor?" The fear in her voice stunned him.

"No, I doubt it. Like I said, cows are pretty tough. It would take more than this to make her lose the calf."

"I'm hungry," Maddie chimed in, pulling out of his embrace and taking Carina by the hand.

The woman shook her head like coming out of a trance. "I hope we can make something edible out of breakfast." Carina's smile looked more like a grimace as Maddie dragged her to the passenger side of the pickup.

He'd grown up on this ranch. His grandfather and then his dad taught him everything he knew about cattle and the land. The ranch and the lifestyle oozed through him like his own blood. He did things instinctively. He knew he'd been gruff with the city woman when she'd balked, but damn it, every cow meant getting out of debt and saving the land and daughter he loved.

Removing the rope halter he'd put on the cow, he could see where some of what they'd just done would look cruel to a city person. And why his mom left the ranch the minute his dad passed away. He rolled up the rope, tossed it in the back of the pickup, and grabbed Tate. The boy picked globs of mud from his hat and threw it toward the cow.

"That's my boy. Put the mud back where it belongs." He set Tate on the seat and slid in behind him as the boy climbed over Maddie to land in Carina's lap.

"Oh, Tate! Now you're just as muddy as the rest of us," she said, with a hint of dismay in her voice.

"We better get back. Jack's bound to be there by now and wondering what we're doing today." Brock turned the key and floored the accelerator, fishtailing the pickup and making Maddie and Tate laugh with glee. He noticed Carina clung to Tate as if they would crash.

After they crossed the cattle guard and were back on the main road, Carina looked at him. "Who is Jack?"

"He's a Basque sheepherder who no longer herds sheep. He works for me as a hired hand."

"It takes more than one person to handle this ranch?" She pushed a muddy strand of hair behind her ear and grimaced.

Brock hid the smile her actions triggered. She was out of her element. But he had to accept she did an admirable job of staying composed.

"There's a thousand acres and four hundred head of cattle to keep an eye on."

"Are all of them going to have babies?" The wonder in her voice made him smile.

"They're called calves, Carina," Maddie said, entering the conversation. The woman smiled at Maddie.

"I stand corrected. Are they all going to have calves?"

"All but the bulls. The more I can keep alive the better." He knew he had to have an above-average number of calves survive to pay off the loan and have enough to get them through the next year. After that, they'd be fine until Maddie and Tate went to college.

But he'd take care of that hurdle when the time came.

"Will they all be born before the snow comes?" He heard the worry in her voice.

"If they go as planned, we should have all the calves on the ground by the end of December."

"But won't you have snow by then?"

"It depends on the year. Some years we don't get it till after the New Year and some years it can start in November. Keep your fingers crossed the snow comes late this year." He tried to give her a reassuring smile, but he could see she didn't buy it.

They pulled into the yard. Jack's Toyota wasn't anywhere to be seen.

Brock got out and looked around. Where could he be? The man hadn't missed a day in ten years.

"Something's wrong." He stomped into the kitchen, banging the door behind him, and tried the phone. Silence.

"Willie T's coming!" Maddie hollered.

Brock went back outside. Carina carried Tate to the house, and Maddie stood by the pickup pointing south. Sure enough, on the horizon he spotted a horse and rider making their way down the small hill. He followed Carina into the kitchen.

"We got company coming. I'll put a pot of coffee on while you and Tate get cleaned up."

"Willie T?" she asked, pulling the muddy coat from Tate.

"Yeah. Maybe he has news about Jack."

"Do they live near one another?"

"No."

"Then how will he have news?"

Brock shrugged. "Willie T just seems to know

everything."

Carina frowned and slipped out of her muddy coat, leaving it in a pile beside the washing machine.

"There's a shower in there," he pointed to the small bathroom in the corner of the mud room. "And a robe to get you up to your clothes," he added. The shy smile on her face as his words sunk in, gave him a glimpse of the real woman. For all her spunk and bossiness, she was bashful. He snorted as she and Tate disappeared into the bathroom. She'd been pretty damn bold staring at him in his shorts the night before. Just remembering her eyes on him hardened a part of his body he'd ignored since Cindy drove away.

Brock wished he had time to clean up before the old Indian arrived, but didn't want to make extra mess by using the upstairs bathroom. He knew if Willie T made the trip to bring information it would take at least two pots of coffee and a big plate of breakfast to get it out of him. That was the least of his worries.

The social service woman planned to come out today to check up on him, thanks to Maxwell. Hell, he wished he knew how to make the bitter man leave this family alone. Willie T was right. Having a nanny would simplify a lot of things in his life.

He rubbed a hand across the tense muscles in his neck. Visions of Carina standing in the mudroom with her rain-soaked clothes clinging to her curvy body and the way her hungry gaze had consumed him last night, had him wishing Willie T had hired an older more haggard nanny.

Four

Carina handed Willie T another cup of coffee as Brock entered the room dressed in clean clothes. His collar-length, black hair was combed back from a tan, sun-etched face. This along with his aristocratic nose and sharp features gave the appearance he could be the old man's Native American son.

"Willie T, now that you've managed to drink a pot of coffee, suppose you tell us what brought you out here?" Brock asked, pouring himself a cup. He brushed against Carina as she moved to place a plate of pancakes on the table alongside the cold plate of bacon and warmed-up scrambled eggs. The tingle his touch elicited set her cheeks on fire. She spun back to the stove to hide her blush.

The old man had barely said a word as he drank coffee and waited for Brock to get cleaned up. He cleared his throat, and Carina turned back to the table interested in what he had to say. Living in a large city, she'd come across all kinds of people from all walks of life, but she'd never met a Native American who lived on the land of his ancestors.

"This coffee is better than usual."

"Willie T you didn't ride that old nag of yours all the way here just for a plate of pancakes and a pot of coffee." Brock set his cup down and leaned on the table staring at the man.

Carina suppressed a giggle. Flustered, Brock had taken the role of the impatient teenager to the older man's elder wisdom. Willie T took another sip of coffee and licked his lips appreciatively, enjoying the limelight.

"Let's eat, then I'll tell you why I rode for two hours to get to my good friends." The twinkle in the man's eyes wasn't lost to Carina. She understood he enjoyed playing with the impatient younger man.

"How about some nice jam to go on those pancakes?" Carina shifted to retrieve a jar of raspberry jam she'd noticed in the refrigerator.

"Now this woman has the right idea. Eat then talk." He smiled at her, showing straight, yellow teeth.

"Willie T! Willie T!" Maddie burst into the kitchen with wet hair soaking her shirt; the mud monster which had entered the shower had returned an exuberant girl.

"Yes, little one?" Softening in Willie T's features gave away his affection for the child. Maddie pushed a chair next to his and sat to his left.

"That storm we was—"

"Were," interrupted Carina.

"That storm we were watching dropped a bunch of rain."

The old man laughed and patted her head. "Yes, it was a bunch of rain." His mouth became grim. He looked at Brock. "The rain caused many washouts." He raised his hand when Brock started to talk. "That is why Jack has not arrived. The road to his place and his daughter's washed out in the canyon. It will be several days before they can dig through the mud."

"What about the road to Halverton?" Brock glanced at Carina and grimaced. "A woman from social services was headed this way today."

Stunned that someone had gone so far as to turn him in to Child Welfare, Carina asked, "Why are they investigating you?"

"It's a long story. But if the road is closed, it will give me time to explain it all after I find the scattered cows."

Carina scanned the faces of the men and the child as they prepared to eat the food on their plates. None of them seemed the least concerned the state wanted to scrutinize their lives. She knew from her experiences as a teacher it could have devastating results for a family.

"How long will it take you to round up the cows?" She wanted answers sooner rather than later.

"Without Jack's help, I'll probably be all day and part of the night. I can't have them getting too far away. It's best to keep them grouped together to watch for early calves and less of a chance to lose one to predators or man."

"Do you need our help?" Carina didn't know the first thing about rounding up cattle, but she could see on his face, it was important.

"When I find them, I could use Maddie's help. The best help you can give is taking care of Tate."

She looked at the smiling toddler and Maddie's sparkling eyes. "I think I can handle that."

"Jack doesn't live that far from us, I don't get—"

Maddie started to say.

"I don't understand." Carina corrected without even thinking.

Maddie sighed. "Do you have to correct everything I say?"

"If I remember right, you corrected me," Carina said, tugging on one of Maddie's braids. She glanced at Brock and Willie T who both hid smiles behind their cups of coffee. "Let's make a pact. You can correct me about ranch terms, and I'll keep helping you with your grammar." She held out her hand to shake. Maddie frowned and glanced at her dad, who nodded his head.

"Okay, but it's kind of annoying." She held out her hand.

Carina's heart swelled at the child's firm grip and exasperated expression.

"What did you want to ask about Jack?" Brock asked.

"Why couldn't he ride a horse like Willie T to get here?" Maddie took a big bite of pancake.

"You need to cut the next bite in half," Carina said, taking a seat in the chair next to Maddie. The girl wrinkled her nose and looked at her dad with pleading eyes.

"You'll do what Carina says while she's with us," he said, grinning. "As for Jack, I'm sure he wants to make sure his family can get out before he comes to help us."

"Oh yeah! His daughter has small children and his mother is real old." Maddie started to take another large bite. Carina cleared her throat. Rolling her eyes, Maddie put the food down and cut it in half.

Willie T burst out laughing. "If I knew having

someone make you be a lady was so much fun, I'd have brought someone here sooner."

Brock turned to Willie T. "Don't think because I gave in to the month that I've forgiven you or Maddie for going behind my back."

Carina felt uncomfortable for the old man and started to get up.

"No, Ms. Valencia, I think you should stay. After all you've been wronged by these two as well. You came here expecting a long-term commitment."

"That's true, but life has a way of throwing lumps in front of me. I'll survive. You shouldn't be too harsh on them. They were looking out for your interests," she said, sitting back down and sending Willie T an apologetic smile.

"They pretended to be me and brought you out here on a lark. If they'd discussed it with me, I could have explained there is no money to hire anyone to help with the housework and Tate." Brock glared at the old man and girl. "Which you should both know since you rifled through my papers to get information for the nanny agency."

"I knew we were on a budget, but I'm willing to give up everything. Clothes, computer games, and school supplies." Maddie pushed her plate away. "Food."

"Don't be ridiculous. You need food or there is no need for a nanny!" Brock shot out of his chair and paced the kitchen. "I know this has been the hardest on you, Maddie. I'd give anything to have someone here full-time to take care of things. But we can't afford anyone, and you know your grandmother won't set foot back at Haven." He stopped at the kitchen sink and looked out the window.

Carina wanted to go to him and comfort. The defiant stance grasping the sink couldn't hide his shoulders sagging with the weight of his troubles.

Brock swung back around, piercing Willie T with his dark gaze. "You're an adult and know better."

"You need adult company, and Maddie shouldn't be Tate's mother." Willie T stared back.

"I know she shouldn't be his mother. She's his sister. But his mother was a worthless bitch."

"Brock!" Carina stood, slapping her hands on the table. "You will not use that kind of language in front of the children." He started to open his mouth. "As long as I'm around here, you will keep such foul things to yourself." She smoothed Tate's blond hair and glared at Brock. "You may have those feelings toward his mother, but you won't say them around him." She looked at Maddie who played with the food on her plate. "Or your daughter."

Brock stared at the woman. She'd only been in his house less than twenty-four hours and she'd already started laying down the rules and telling what he could and couldn't do. He opened his mouth to protest, but all the things he wanted to say seemed childish considering what had popped out of his mouth moments before. He shook himself mentally. She was protecting his children – from him. He walked over to Maddie.

"Sorry, Freckles, I didn't mean to have it come out like that." He patted her head and leaned over to kiss the top of Tate's head. "Sorry, pal." He didn't even look at the woman who was turning this family into something civilized.

"Come on," he said to Willie T and headed into the

mud room for his coat and boots.

"Thank you for the breakfast, Ms. Valencia."

"Call me Carina." He heard the woman say from the kitchen.

"Carina. I'm glad both you and the rain came. This family needed both." Willie T joined him in the mud room.

"Why'd you go and say that?" Brock straightened from tying his Packers.

"It's the truth." Willie T shrugged. "You and the children do need her. Before she arrived, anyone would have done, but after seeing her defend your children, she is the one you need."

Brock glared at the old man. He didn't need anyone and especially not the woman in the kitchen. His nether regions roared to life thinking of needing her. He growled and tamped down the desire that surged when he thought of her curves and crooked smile.

"Come help me check the herd. We already had to pull a cow out of a dip this morning."

Willie T tipped his head toward the kitchen. "She help?"

"If you could call it that." Brock snorted and headed out the door with Willie T right behind him. "She's a city girl. Maddie had to tell her what a calf was."

"But she pitched in and helped?"

"Yeah." Brock thought of her pushing on the cow and rushing to save her when she realized the pickup would pull on the animal's hocks. "She isn't afraid of dirt and helping."

"That's good. She may need to help you more until

Jack can get here." Willie T climbed into the passenger side of the pickup.

Brock didn't like the idea of relying on Carina and Maddie to help him with the cows, but he didn't have a choice. "Could you come over every day and help?" he asked the old man.

He grinned and shook his head. "Got family who need me."

"How did they fair with the rains?" Brock knew Willie T didn't have a lot of his family left. A couple of kids and some grandchildren, his wife and siblings had left this earth some years ago.

"The kids and grandkids, all but two, have no problems, but I'll have to help the ones whose roads did wash out. I'm going after supplies tomorrow."

"Did the monthly shipment get to Dutch Springs before all the washouts?"

"Yeah, we will all have plenty until another shipment arrives."

"Good, I plan to head down there for supplies in a couple of days." Brock thought of Carina trying to call her friend. "Ms. Valencia could get a signal on her cell phone from there if the phones don't make it back on."

"She got family to contact?" Willie T seemed to finally take an interest in the conversation.

"I don't know. She called a friend last night to say she arrived." Last night he hadn't wanted to learn anything about the woman. After witnessing the sadness in her eyes and her fierce loyalty to his children, he wanted to know everything he could about the woman.

"Boyfriend?"

A wave of jealousy, something he hadn't felt since

dating Beth, surged through him. "I don't think so. She's coming off a rough divorce."

"I see."

He could almost see the wheels cranking behind Willie T's rheumy eyes. "Whatever you see. Keep me out of it."

The old man nodded his head, but the twinkle in his eyes told Brock he'd better be wary. There was no way the old man and his daughter would get him hooked up with another woman. He had Beth's love to sustain him through this life and didn't want someone messing up his family. Mentally, he knew this was how it should be, but his body reacted differently to the idea of Ms. Valencia taking care of his kids and sashaying around the house.

Five

Carina had lunch on the table when the two men returned.

"It looks good, Ms. Valencia," Willie T said, taking a seat at the table.

"Please, I asked you to call me Carina." She placed a cup of coffee in front of him while Brock scrounged around in a cupboard. "Do you need something I forgot?" she asked.

He pulled a large thermos out of the cupboard. "No, but I'd appreciate it if you'd put together about five or six sandwiches. There's still some cows missing. Maddie and I'll head out as soon as you get those ready."

Maddie jumped up and helped make the sandwiches, while Brock poured all the coffee from the pot into the thermos and started another pot.

Once the sandwiches were made, Maddie grabbed her hat and coat, following her father out the door. Carina cleaned up the mess after Willie T ate three sandwiches, washing them down with another pot of coffee.

"I need to head over to my daughter's. They had some rain damage, and I promised to get supplies for them tomorrow." Willie T scooted his chair back from the table and stood.

"It was good of you to inform us of the washed-out roads and help Brock look for cattle this morning." Carina picked up the dishes.

"This family is like my own flesh-n-blood." He grinned and patted her shoulder. "You, too."

Carina stared at the man's back as he left the room. When the back door clicked shut, she peered at Tate. "What are we going to do with our afternoon?"

***

Carina found herself looking for things to do after she put Tate down for a nap. She'd never been one to sit and do nothing. After digging around, she found a rag and dusted the antiques about the house. This small chore reminded her of afternoons spent in her mother's antique shop.

She carefully cleaned the creases in the carvings on the grandfather clock and wondered if Brock's great-grandfather had carved the date in it anywhere. Growing up with an antique dealer had imparted her with a love of the old pieces and an interest in their history.

Opening the door on the front of the clock, she ran her fingers over the base to see if a date had been carved. Her hand bumped something. A wave of conscience stalled her hand, but her curiosity won, and she closed her fingers around a small bundle of letters held together by a hardening rubber band.

She rippled the end of the bundle with her thumb.

It would be an invasion of privacy to read them. She turned the bundle over. They were addressed to Beth Johnson in a man's square lettering. She looked at the return address. An APO address. Military. Tapping the letters against her palm, she battled with her inquisitiveness.

Wasn't Beth the name of Brock's first wife? Maddie's mother. From the brief dossier the agency handed her, she knew Brock served in the military.

Presuming Brock and Maddie wouldn't arrive back at the house until after dark, she sat down on the couch and slowly rolled the drying rubber band down the bundle. The band snapped, scattering the letters across the floor.

Carina fell to her knees, scooping the envelopes into a pile. One by one, she read the postmark dates. The letters spanned a couple of years. If Brock wrote them what could it hurt for her to read a little bit about his past? Maybe it might help her understand the man and his family better.

She tapped the letter in the palm of her hand. If he sent it to his first wife, it was personal. She bit her lip. Would she want someone reading something she wrote to someone she loved? Someone who was dead and still loved?

No.

Gnawing on her lip didn't squelch the desire to know more about the man.

She wanted to see what made Brock love his first wife so deeply he couldn't love another. From the name he called his second wife this morning, it sounded like there had been little love between them. Her chest tightened with sadness. The thought reaffirmed her mother's words. She'd always said she would never be able to love another man as she had Carina's father, who died much too young leaving behind a wife and daughter.

If Brock and Beth had shared such a love, she wished to learn more. From her failed marriage, it was unlikely she'd ever experience such a love in her life. At first, she'd thought Perry was her one true love. However, his need to move up the corporate ladder and his less-than-attentive nature after the miscarriage proved he never loved her unconditionally.

She slipped the single sheet of paper out of an envelope postmarked March 1991 and stared at the square penmanship covering the page.

Beth,

I miss you and the sagebrush and sandy soil of that damned land of my family with such a longing it nearly makes me sick. Why did I sign up for military duty when I have you waiting for me? At the time, I felt it was something I needed to do, but sitting here in the heat, staring at a photo of you, I wish you had talked me out of it. I love you. When I get done with this tour, I'm coming for you, and we're going to get married. I don't care what your dad thinks of me. We belong together. We love the dry, god-forsaken country of our families and each other. What more do we need?

Love always,
Brock

Carina wiped at the tear trickling down her cheek. He wasn't poetic, but she could imagine the love welling in the heart of the young woman reading the letter.

So Beth's family lived around here. Why weren't they helping with the rearing of their granddaughter? Brock had written her father didn't like him. Surely, once the two were married and he saw how much the man loved his daughter they made amends? She'd ask Maddie about her mother's family.

The far-off bark of a dog surprised her. The only dog that barked around here was Roscoe, and he'd left in the back of the truck with Brock and Maddie.

They were back. Fear of being found with the letters set her in motion. She bundled the envelopes into her hands and hurried across the room to the clock. She set the bundle in the back of the clock and they tumbled over. Shoot! Would he notice there wasn't a rubber band? Did she have time to find another one? The rumble of a motor suggested not.

Taking a deep breath, she shut the clock with a click and gathered her dusting supplies. Carina walked casually down the hall with the dust rag in her hand. Maddie burst through the back door as Carina flipped the rag at a cobweb in a corner of the hallway. The girl plopped her backside down on the bench in the mudroom.

"We found them!" she shouted, kicking off her rubber boots and pulling on a pair of cowboy boots.

"The cows?" Carina asked, placing the dust rag and spray in the cupboard. She took a deep breath to compose herself and slow her frantically beating heart. Deceit had never been a part of her life. Not until she'd been left with empty arms and no home.

"Yeah, they're over on the bluffs. Gotta use the horses." Maddie headed for the door.

"But it's just about dinner time and nearly dark."

"No time. They haven't had much feed."

Carina grabbed the child by her coat before she darted out the door. "Where's your dad?"

"In the barn. Saddling the horses."

Pulling a coat off a hook, she followed the girl out to the large building she had yet to explore.

She'd grown up in the city dreaming of horses, dogs, and the wide-open spaces. This was her chance to fulfill her dreams. Brock was tightening a leather strap on a horse when she entered the building behind Maddie.

"You get in and out without that city woman seeing you?" Brock asked, not turning from his task.

She stared at the man as he continued deftly working with the horse. Did he call her the city woman all the time around Maddie? That was demeaning in itself without his trying to hide their actions from her.

"No, she didn't," Carina answered. His head jerked around at the sound of her voice. The guilty look on his face made her laugh. "Why didn't you want me to know you were headed God knows where right before dark to get cows?"

"Because you'd come out here and debate and waste time." He strode across the space between the horses and bridles hanging on the wall.

"Is it wise to put your lives at risk to go after cows who will be in the same spot tomorrow morning when you have a full day of light to gather them?" Carina moved closer as he put the headgear on the horse. She couldn't resist reaching out and touching the animal. The thrill it brought her was new and welcome. She pet the horse and inhaled deeply, breathing in the animal, leather, and the man standing within arm's reach.

"You allergic to horses?" he asked, walking the animal away from her.

"No, I've never been this close to one before. I've read in books how people who like horses love the scent of leather and the animal, but until this moment I never knew what they were talking about." She snickered when Brock stared at her like she needed a tranquilizer.

"You've never been near a horse?" Maddie chimed in, leading a horse toward them with such authority it made Carina a bit jealous to think she had never had the chance to see if she could control an animal. The girl stood in front of her handling the large animal with the same confidence she handled her brother.

"Never." Carina placed a hand on the soft nose of the horse Maddie held. "But I'd love to ride one." She glanced at Brock.

"You won't be riding one here. We don't have time to teach you." He led the horse out of the barn and next to a trailer hooked onto his pickup.

"I would think living in country like this it would be a necessity to know how to ride." Carina crossed her arms and stared at the man.

"I told you there's no time." He opened the door of the trailer and led the horse in.

"I don't mean right this minute. I'll be here a month at least."

He stopped and stared at her. "Only a month."

"I would think in that month you could find a spare moment here or there to show me the basics in case you need me to help."

"In case you haven't noticed, this is a cattle ranch.

There are incidents all the time that take up my time, and I'm one hand short."

"I would think Maddie could—"

He chopped her sentence off with a dark look and his hand slicing through the air. "No! She won't give you lessons. A greenhorn like you on a horse is dangerous." He motioned toward the interior of the trailer. "Maddie, get your horse in there."

When Maddie and the horse walked inside, he stepped so close to Carina she could feel his breath on her forehead. She peered into his anger-filled eyes.

"Do not ask Maddie to teach you."

"Why?"

"I have my reasons." The agony she saw behind the anger tore at her. Something tormented him.

"Fine. I won't ask her. But I still think it's crazy to move cows in the dark." Carina backed away from the man and her need to reach out to him and try to ease the suffering she saw in his eyes.

"We don't have far to move them, but I want them in feed as soon as possible. This is an important time for the growth of the calves in their bellies." He shut the door on the trailer and hurried back into the barn.

"Be careful," Carina told Maddie as the girl climbed into the cab of the truck.

"We'll be fine. We both know the area and the horses have done this a hundred times."

Her youthful optimism made Carina smile.

Brock returned with four flashlights. "You don't happen to have anything in the house we can take along to snack on do you?" he asked.

"Did you already eat all those sandwiches?" The sheepish look on his face answered her question. "I made cookies before Tate went down for a nap." She hurried into the house and filled a bag with cookies. Turning to hurry back out to the truck, she nearly ran into Brock.

"Sorry, for being so harsh out there, but I've got a lot on my mind," his deep voice softened with apology while his eyes watched her.

"I'll forgive you this time, but I'm not giving up on the lessons." Carina held up the bag of cookies. "Be careful."

He looked in the bag and licked his lips. "Chocolate chip. My favorite, I don't know if Maddie will get any."

"If she doesn't you have to give me lessons," Carina said as he turned and hurried out the door.

She didn't know when they would return. Running to the door, she threw it open and yelled, "When do you think you'll be back?"

Brock waved and kept on going.

They'd get soup whenever they came home. She returned to the house, removed her coat, and headed up the stairs to see if Tate was awake.

Walking to the boy's room, she thought of Brock's aversion to her learning to ride. What could possibly happen if he rode right beside her showing her what to do? She knew riding alone could be dangerous. She'd read more than one story about a lone rider either dying or becoming crippled from a fall. But why was he so adamant about not teaching her?

Tate stood in his crib a smile on his round, cherub face.

"Hey, big boy, you ready to keep me company? Your dad and sister have left us alone for a while longer. She picked him up, enjoying the weight and his legs wrapping around her body. He placed his hands on either side of her face and laid a loud, sloppy kiss on her nose. If she hadn't already lost her heart to the boy the night before, his sweet kiss would have done it now. Tears trickled down her cheeks. She would never relish the sweetness of her own child's kiss. The ache this knowledge brought to her chest, took her breath away.

Tate smiled at her and touched the tears. Holding him, cleaving to his innocence, she slowly regained control of the moment. But she knew each day spent with him would make it harder to leave when the month ended. It would be like losing her child all over again.

After changing his diaper, she rested him on her hip and headed down the stairs. When Maddie gave her a tour of the house the day before, she noticed a bookcase full of books on cattle and horses in the office. She strode into Brock's sanctuary, plucked a book on the basics of horse riding, and settled into a large overstuffed chair. Maybe if she showed some knowledge of the animal and riding, Brock would take her request more serious.

***

Brock and Maddie rolled into the yard around midnight. Carina met them at the barn.

"Go take a hot shower. I have soup on the stove," she told Maddie, taking the rope from her hands and leading her horse to a hitching post.

Maddie glanced at her dad and then at Carina. "It's okay, I think I can unsaddle your horse." Carina shooed the girl out of the barn.

"This isn't going to get you riding lessons," Brock said, loosening the cinch on his horse.

"Did you get the cattle moved?" she asked, changing the subject and mimicking everything he did. While reading the books on horses, she'd decided to go at this differently. Act as if she didn't want to learn to ride, but help as much as she could with the animals.

"Yeah, they're all accounted for and together. Makes it a whole lot easier to keep an eye on them when they aren't scattered." He pulled the saddle from the horse's back and packed it to a rack on the wall.

Carina had the cinch loose, but wasn't sure what to do with it. She flopped it over the saddle and grasped the two ends of the saddle, dragging it down off the horse. After watching Brock, she hadn't expected the thing to weigh so darn much. Gravity took over and the saddle landed with a thud on her feet.

Her face heated with embarrassment. She quickly picked the saddle up and lugged it to the rack.

"Let me help you." Brock's hands touched hers when he grasped the saddle.

Electricity shot up her arms from his touch. She stepped back as he placed the saddle on the rack. Had he felt the charge? He didn't appear to be flustered. Her heart thudded in her chest like a runaway horse.

Brock took a minute straightening the stirrups and cinches on the saddles before turning back to the woman. He didn't want her to see how her touch affected him. It had been a long time since a woman set off bolts of need through him. And the brunette who'd taken over his house did.

"You said something about soup?" He walked over to the horses, untying each one and leading them to the stalls in the barn.

"I put chicken soup on low about two hours ago.

You never said when you'd be back." The accusation in her voice made him grin.

"When I'm chasing cattle, I never know when I'll be back."

"It's a good thing Maddie doesn't go to school. Keeping her out till midnight would make it hard for her to get up in the morning."

Again, with the accusing tone.

He knew someone from the city didn't understand the urgency of his actions where the cattle were concerned, but damn, she didn't have to act as if he were a neglectful parent.

"If you hadn't been here to watch Tate, Maddie would have been in the house and in bed when I came home." He unbuckled the halters on the horses and let them go.

"So you think leaving a twelve-year-old alone for hours at night with her baby brother is better than taking her with you?" Her cheeks flushed, her eyes glistened with indignation.

"You have no right to come here and criticize how I raise my children." He took three long strides toward her. "Do they look abused or neglected to you?" Towering over her, he glared at her upturned face. How dare she question him?

She didn't back away or down.

"Your daughter ordering a nanny screams of neglect to me," Carina retorted with steel in her voice.

Her reaction puzzled him.

"She had help." He did feel remorse his daughter knew what she needed and he didn't.

"But you knew nothing about it." She threw her hands in the air, turned away, then swung back around.

"If you supervised your children as you say you do, she wouldn't have been able to arrange for a nanny and have one arrive without your knowledge."

She was right, but he'd never admit it. He was a bad excuse for a father. He loved the land and his children and was torn between the two. They both needed him.

Brock rubbed a hand over his face and backed away from the woman who made him see himself in an unfavorable light. "I know," he mumbled.

"You know what?" she stepped close. He could smell her perfume and the scent of baby powder.

"I know I'm not around enough, but they also need fed and clothed and this god-forsaken land is what puts food on the table and clothes on their backs."

"But they need you, too." Her expression softened. "Physical contact is just as important as food and shelter." She reached out, rubbing his arm. "You're a wonderful father when you're with the children. And I've no doubt Maddie had a terrific time with you today."

The energy her touch set off frightened him. God help him. Between the zing of her touch and the passion in her words, his body overruled his good sense.

Grasping her shoulders, he pulled her against his chest, breathing in her arousing scent. It felt good to hold a woman again. Especially, one who'd just given him such high praise, even if it was after raking him up one side and down the other.

When she didn't pull from his embrace, he slid his hand down her back, forgetting all the reasons he'd built to stay away from a woman.

"Daddy! Carina! Are you coming in soon?"

Maddie called from the house.

Carina stepped out of his arms and ducked her head as she headed to the door of the barn.

Brock wasn't sure if he needed to apologize for holding her or for being a poor father. "I'm sorry," he said just when she reached the door.

She looked back. From the distance, he couldn't see what flared in her eyes. "You have no need to apologize. I'm the one who started demeaning you. I'm sorry. You're a good man. You only have to tolerate my rages for a month. Then I'll be out of your life." She jogged to the house.

Brock flipped the lights off in the barn and stood in the dark. Out of your life. He didn't want her out of his life. She was good for the kids. He relived holding her in his arms. Contentment flowed through him mixed with desire.

And good for him. When the month was up, he'd find a way to pay her to stay on.

Six

Brock dropped his reading glasses on top of the
ledger and rubbed his temples. He had to get top dollar
for every calf and possibly sell a couple of cows to get
out from under the bank's thumb. It still rankled Ray
bailed on him, taking a job in a larger city and leaving
him at the mercy of the head of the local bank. The
bank manager had high hopes to repossess the ranch
and resell for big money—leaving his family homeless.

Strains of Shania Twain vibrated the windows in
the office as the bass of the song shook the house.

"What the…" He pushed back from the desk and
stood. Shania Twain didn't bother him, but the decibels
set his hair dancing. Brock crossed the room in two
strides.

At the kitchen door, he heard his daughter's young
voice and the deep, sultry tones he recognized as
Carina's, boom out the words, "I feel like a woman".

Leaning against the doorjamb, he couldn't help but
smile.

Carina and Maddie sang into wooden spoons and

shook their backsides like a horse scratching its tail on a tree. Watching the slow sway of Carina's hips sent heat to his loins. Her seductive voice curled around him, drowning out Shania and the world in general.

She tossed her hair over her shoulder and glanced back. Spotting him, her face flushed, but she kept on singing with Maddie sidestepping alongside her. They both shouted the last sentence, "Man, I feel like a woman!" and broke into laughter.

Seeing the joy on Maddie's face made his heart thud with happiness. She was his light and grounded him. It melted his heart seeing her act like a kid. With all her responsibilities, she rarely let herself go.

Clapping his hands, he moved into the room. Maddie jumped as though she'd been caught doing something wrong.

"We were—"

"Having fun. There's nothing wrong with that." He tweaked her freckled nose and looked at the flushed face and sparkling eyes of Carina. "I'm surprised a city girl knows how to belt out Shania." He kept his gaze on the woman, appreciating the sparkling eyes and high color.

"She's a crossover artist." Carina flipped the radio off.

"Crossover?" He hadn't a clue what she meant.

"Her music is played on country and pop stations," Carina explained.

"Ah. So you listen to pop music?"

"When I can. My husband only listened to classical and thought that was all that should be played in the house." She pushed her dark brown hair behind her ear. "He thought my listening to culture would make me more acceptable in his circle."

The wail of Tate waking from a nap pulled her angry gaze from his face. That was the first insight she'd given him to her previous marriage, and he found it interesting.

"I'll get Tate." She handed her spoon to Maddie. "Give your dad some cookies," she added, leaving the room.

Brock followed her departure with his gaze. She was all woman coming or going and after watching the sway of her hips when she sang, it was a scene that would remain branded on his mind.

A tug on his shirt drew his attention back to the kitchen. "Don't be mad at Carina." Maddie's worried voice startled him.

"Why should I be mad?" He sat at the table while she placed a plate of cookies before him and a cup of coffee.

"We had the radio loud and were goofing around."

Had he been so hard on his daughter she felt she couldn't have fun? *Damn*.

"Honey, never apologize for having fun as long as it doesn't hurt anyone or interfere with your work."

She threw her arms around his neck and looked at him with tears glistening in her eyes. "Don't send Carina away at the end of the month. She's fun and helps me learn things I can't get from a book."

He was just as torn about their nanny. "I'm trying to find a way to keep her. So let me worry about it." He bit a cookie and wrinkled his nose. "This tastes funny."

"We've run out of a lot of stuff so we experimented."

"That reminds me. I plan to go to Dutch Springs

this afternoon. You interested in tagging along?"

His daughter's eyes lit up. "You know I would. Rayanne lives there!" Maddie hugged him tight and danced around the kitchen.

"What's this all about?" Carina entered the kitchen with Tate on her hip.

Brock envied his son. He'd like to be the one riding…

"We're going to Dutch Springs this afternoon!" Maddie offered, pulling Brock away from the sensual images of his thoughts.

"Oh! Is it a big town?"

Maddie laughed and looked at him.

"No, it's a community of about twenty people. There's a grocery store, gas station, and restaurant." Brock didn't miss the look of fascination that twinkled in Carina's eyes.

"Do they have phone service?" Carina placed Tate in his highchair and carefully strapped in his wiggly body.

"Probably not, but you should be able to use your cell phone. They are a little higher and have a cell tower to the south of them." Brock stood. "I figure if we leave right after lunch, we can get there about two, get the groceries, fill up with gas, grab an early dinner, and head home."

"It takes that long to get there? Wouldn't it be closer to go to Halverton?"

"It usually only takes about forty-five minutes, but Willie T said all the roads are treacherous due to the rain."

"Oh, so it'll be an adventure." Her face lit up.

"I guess you could call it that." Brock scratched his

head and stared at the woman. Was there nothing she could find a silver lining to?

She moved about the kitchen, preparing the noon meal. He knew he should get back to the books, but watching her filled him with contentment.

"Maddie, will you open a can of tuna and fix it, please," Carina said, smiling at the girl. Maddie jumped into action.

The bond between Carina and Maddie made him smile. They respected one another. He'd seen few women show the kind of respect to children that Carina did. She said her marriage ended due to health reasons. Was that why she'd never had any children? Her actions proved she'd make a wonderful mother and an exceptional wife. What kind of jerk had she married? *Easy, man.* There's no need to be jealous of someone who isn't around. Especially, when you have no designs on ever marrying, again.

"Do you have brothers and sisters?" he asked, knowing she didn't like to talk about herself, but maybe she'd talk about her family.

"No. You?" She placed a loaf of bread on the table and returned to the counter.

"No. What about your parents? Are they still alive?" He saw her shoulders relax as she dumped chips into a bowl.

The look of love and serenity in her eyes when she turned to the table told him she thought highly of her parents.

"My mother is. She buys and sells antiques."

"What about your father?"

The brightness in her eyes faded. "He died when I was young."

"Your mother never remarried?" He empathized with a woman he'd never met. He never should have thought he could remarry after the love he and Beth shared.

"No. After my dad died, she put all her love and passion into me and antiques." The sadness in her voice perplexed him.

"Why does that make you sad?"

She looked up from her task. "I don't want to go into it now." The pain in her eyes made his heart ache.

"Why?"

She glanced away. "It's personal."

Maddie touched his shoulder and shook her head. He grabbed his daughter and hugged her. When had she become so sensitive to others?

"What did your mother think of you coming out here to be a nanny?" he asked, changing the subject.

Her face colored, and her eyes dulled before she spun to retrieve something from the refrigerator.

"She wondered about my career change." Carina knew she'd let her feelings show briefly by the way he stared at her. Her mother had been devastated by the miscarriage and then her only child rushing out of her life. Carina hadn't wanted to hurt her mother, but she couldn't move on with the woman constantly monitoring her every movement and comment. A person could only take, 'It's because of your loss you're saying this, or doing this' before it made you feel crazy.

"Did she accept it or are you running?" His direct question hit her like a smack to the head. She grabbed the pickles out of the refrigerator and placed them on the table with a solid thud.

"She has never questioned any of my decisions.

But she wasn't thrilled with my leaving." She glanced around. "Where are your parents? Or the children's other grandparents for that matter? They could help watch Maddie and Tate."

She saw the hint of anger flash in his eyes before he grabbed the loaf of bread and started dealing slices out on the plates like a card shark.

"My father passed away ten years ago. After his funeral, my mother packed her things and moved to Florida with her sister."

"Did you ask her to come back and help with your children?"

He glared at her and nodded toward Maddie, indicating he didn't want to talk about it with the girl present.

"It's okay Daddy. I know Grandma doesn't want to come here. Rayanne's grandma told me how much Grandma hated it here." Maddie peered at Carina and shrugged. "My grandma hated this country. Rayanne's grandma said she tried to be friends with her, but Grandma didn't want any kind of relationship that bound her to this land other than her husband." She looked at her father. "Sorry, Daddy." She bowed her head.

"It's okay, Freckles. You can't help how your Grandma felt about the land." He looked at Carina. "My mother and father met at college. It was the only time in his life my father left this ranch. My grandfather wanted him to see the world before he made the decision to live here." He scoffed. "I guess he loved the land so much he made it sound like Eden to my mother. They married before she'd set foot here. Right after the honeymoon they moved into this house with my grandparents. I don't have any siblings because I was conceived on their honeymoon. Before she felt like a prisoner." He ran a hand through his hair. Carina could see even though he spoke of this with as little emotion as possible, his mother abandoning him and the ranch hurt him deeply.

"My appearance made any more children out of the question. By then, I was one more commitment she didn't want. As Rayanne's grandma stated, she didn't want anything to hold her to this land. When my father was out late, she didn't wait up for him. I think she secretly hoped something would happen to him. She hated it out here as much as my father loved it."

"Why didn't she just get a divorce?" Carina wouldn't have stayed somewhere she loathed.

"Her father told her she would be sorry to marry a desert rancher. They never got along, and she wasn't about to go home to him or admit he'd been right." Brock shook his head. "Eat. Let's not let a conversation about my mother ruin our afternoon."

Carina knew he was hurting and embarrassed. She wouldn't push for more now. She'd find another time to try and sooth his feeling of abandonment. First his mother leaving and not looking back, his first wife dying, and his second wife running, it was enough to make even a strong man like Brock have issues.

She and Brock ate in silence while Maddie kept a one-sided dialogue going about her friend Rayanne and the community of Dutch Springs.

"The restaurant is run by Rayanne's mom and dad. They mostly get locals, but every once in a while, someone will drive through and stop for a meal. Everyone comes to her grandma for answers to everything. She's related to Willie T, but I've never asked how. Then there's the gas station. Rayanne's uncle owns and runs the gas station. He's kind of grumpy." Her nose wrinkled. "And the motel is run by Rayanne's aunt and uncle. They're real nice. We stayed there once when there was a bad storm came in after we got there." She looked at Brock. "Do you remember that, Daddy?"

He nodded, but the look in his eyes told Carina it was an event he wanted to forget. Making her all the more curious about the event and the man.

"Why were you at Dutch Springs?" she asked, hoping Brock wouldn't cut Maddie off.

"We'd come back from Mommy's funeral and needed supplies, so we drove straight to Dutch Springs instead of stopping here and spending the night and going on in the morning."

Carina picked at the crust on her bread. He had avoided coming home to a house full of memories. She could understand that. "If the storm hit without notice it was a good thing you went straight for supplies instead of getting here with nothing to eat."

"Yeah, I think Mommy told us to get supplies first. Not wanting us to be home and starving." Maddie looked at Brock. "That's what you said, huh, Daddy?"

"Yeah, Freckles. Mommy looks after us." His voice cracked with emotion, and he didn't look up from his plate. "I'm going to get the fuel barrel loaded in the pickup. Clean up and be ready to go in fifteen minutes," he said, pushing back from the table, avoiding eye contact. He stood, walking out of the room so fast you'd have thought it caught fire.

Maddie shifted her sad eyes to Carina. "He misses

her too much." She stood, gathering the dishes from the table. "Cindy told him he'd never love anyone but his dead wife." She sought Carina's gaze. "I know he loved Mommy for a long time before they married, but I think he could love someone else. He tells me he has enough love in his heart for both Tate and me, so why shouldn't he have enough for another wife?"

Carina hugged the wise girl. "He does, he just hasn't accepted it yet. Sometimes when you love someone as much as your father loved your mother it takes a while for them to let someone else in."

"I hope he lets someone in soon. He's lonely." Maddie pulled out of her embrace, putting the dishes in the sink.

Carina had to agree. He was a lonely man who would make an excellent husband. She thought of their embrace in the barn. Her body warmed just thinking of his strong arms around her. She was sure he would be an excellent husband in every way.

A horn blasted and Maddie squealed, "He didn't give us time to wash the dishes!"

"Get your coat and tell him to hold on. I'll get Tate's shoes and coat and my phone." Carina hauled Tate out of the highchair and carried him upstairs to gather his shoes, coat, and diaper bag. Then she hurried to her room to collect her cell phone. Hearing Georgie's voice would help her find perspective and let her friend know she was still here and surviving.

The horn blasted again. Carina rolled her eyes. The man could be so impatient when he tried to run from his past. The more she learned about him, she understood why he kept to himself. It was how he avoided pain. If he didn't put himself out there no one could hurt him.

She headed down the stairs being careful not to slip. Tate wiggled in her arms, drawing from the excitement of something happening.

"BEEP! BEEP!"

"I'm coming," she muttered under her breath, grabbing her coat from the rack in the mud room. She pulled the back door shut behind her and wondered how to lock it.

"Hey!" She hollered at Brock who stood beside the truck talking to a man sitting in a smaller version.

He glanced up, smiled, and waved her over.

She shook her head. "How do I lock the door?"

"You don't. Come meet Jack."

She rolled her eyes and walked over to where Brock stood talking to a man who appeared not much larger than Maddie.

"Carina Valencia, this is Jack Barreda. He helps me keep this place in the black."

"Pleased to meet you, Mr. –"

"Please, call me Jack." He flashed a smile full of large, white teeth.

"Then you must call me Carina." She faced Brock. "You really should get a lock for your doors."

He smiled and spoke to Jack. "I'm glad your family is dug out and you're back. Check out the cows down by the spring. We're headed for supplies. See you tomorrow." He squeezed Jack's arm and motioned for Carina to get in the truck.

His nonchalance about the valuables in his house irked her. She briskly walked to the passenger side of the truck and set Tate over the front seat into the car seat. When Brock was behind the wheel and started the vehicle, she couldn't hold her thoughts any longer.

Sprawled over the back of the seat, sliding Tate's feet into his shoes, she said, "You have thousands of dollars of antiques in there. You should lock your house."

"You mean all that old furniture?" Brock shoved the gear stick into first and headed out the driveway. Carina nearly flopped into the back. She pushed her body up and took a seat in the front, glaring at Brock.

"Most of that 'old furniture' is over a hundred years old and in excellent condition. There are a lot of collectors out there who would pay top dollar for nearly everything in your house."

"And you know this how?"

"I told you, my mother buys and sells antiques. I've spent many summers and weekends helping in her shop." She stared over Maddie's head to watch Brock. "The Grandfather clock would bring in as much as forty of your calves."

He stared at her until Maddie yelped, causing him to wrench on the steering wheel to bring the truck back on the road.

"That clock is worth forty thousand?"

"That's a low estimate, but at the right auction or shop, you would get top dollar."

He narrowed his eyes. "You aren't just trying to get your mother some work?"

"No!" The nerve of the man, thinking she was scouting for her mother. "I'm just making you see the need for locks on your doors." She folded her arms and settled into the seat. All she wanted to do was help, not hock his family heirlooms.

Brock stared at the road, running figures over in his head. He hadn't parted with the old furniture over the years because it was easier to keep it than try and find anything to replace it.

But several pieces just took up space. He watched Carina out of the corner of his eye. Would she be willing to take some of the pieces as payment? It would keep her on a few more months, which would make Maddie happy. And after all, she was the one who brought Carina to them and deserved to have the pleasure of her companionship.

Carina pushed her thick hair behind her tiny ear. The sight warmed him not with desire but a healthy glow. He'd try whatever it took to get her to stay longer. She was the first woman in a long time he felt at ease around. Sure, she put him in his place when he deserved it and even when he didn't, but it wasn't out of spite, it was because she wanted what was best for his children.

"Daddy!"

Seven

Brock jerked his attention back to the road in time to avoid burying the bumper in a mudslide. "Thanks, Freckles," He squeezed Maddie's leg before putting the pickup in reverse. When he had the vehicle headed down the road again, he glanced at Carina.

"Would you be willing to stay on as nanny for some of those antiques?" He held his breath when she continued to stare forward. He finally had to return his gaze to the road to keep from sliding off the edge.

"Are you saying you're willing to sell your family's heirlooms to have me stay on as your children's nanny?"

"If you'll accept some of the antiques until I can pay you the right way."

"How long do you think that will be?"

He stared over Maddie's head. Carina watched him intently.

"Until I get the calves sold next September."

"So basically, a year of paying for my services with antiques."

He shrugged. "The idea just came to me. I haven't had time to think it through."

"Well, think it through because it isn't me you pay, but the nanny agency. I don't think they'll be interested in antiques as payment." She stared at the road in front of them.

Maddie squirmed beside him and tugged on his sleeve. He glanced down at her, and she wrinkled her nose in a conspiring grin. Brock smiled back and knew with her help they'd find a way to turn the antiques into money to pay the nanny agency.

They made better time than he'd expected. Brock spotted Dutch Springs at a quarter to two in the afternoon. Maddie wiggled in the seat next to him.

"Hold on. Your squirming won't get us there any faster," he said, watching Carina. He had to smile at the excitement sparkling in the woman's eyes.

"Why is this called a community rather than a town?" she asked, scanning the few buildings along the road. He pulled into the gas station and switched the ignition off.

"They aren't incorporated. No post office, mayor, or anything official. Just a family trying to stay alive without relying on Mother Nature and the land." Brock opened his door and pointed to the grocery. "It's a small store, but they stock it well knowing we don't have time to go the distance to the bigger stores. You go on over and start gathering what we need." He tugged on Maddie's braid. "Go on and find Rayanne. We'll meet you at the restaurant when we're ready to eat." Maddie crawled over him and disappeared in a flash.

Carina laughed. "How often does she get to see her

friends?"

"More often than it looks, believe me." He stretched his arms toward Carina to take Tate.

"He's fine. I'll take him with me." Carina slid out of the vehicle and propped Tate on her hip. She turned to Brock. The expression on his face sent tendrils of heat swirling in her. His eyes blazed with desire while his lips curved in a content smile.

"You make a sight, Ms. Valencia," he said in a low, seductive voice.

Carina spun and walked quickly toward the store. Where had that come from? First, he offered her antiques to stay on and just now… Heat surged from her center to her toes and fingers at his words and the desire in his eyes. How could she continue to be a nanny in his house? Before she knew it, she'd be begging him to kiss her. Or worse—taking things into her own hands and kissing him.

She shoved the door of the small store open and focused her mind on getting groceries. Tate was fully awake and squirming to get down.

"Oh no, you don't. You'll have everything off the shelves." Glancing around, she hunted for a shopping cart. In the very back she spotted a rather old rickety contraption that once could have been a shopping cart.

A woman near her age stood behind the counter. She had platinum-dyed hair with dark roots and thick makeup which would rival Elvira's. Her plaid flannel shirt stretched across an ample girth while her stick legs were encased in spandex leggings.

"Is that thing safe?" Carina asked, pointing at the shopping cart.

"He's been in it before and it hasn't collapsed,"

said the woman, eyeing her up and down.

Carina ignored the jab and moved off to gather her groceries. The woman came out from behind the counter and followed them up and down the aisles.

"You aren't a relation to Brock. What bar did he pick you up in?" she asked as Carina put a box of dry milk in the cart.

"I don't spend time at bars," she answered, hoping the woman would leave her alone.

"Brock only comes here or goes to the bar in Halverton. I haven't seen you around here, so he had to have come across you at the bar in Halverton."

"Sorry to disappoint you. But he didn't come across me at any bar." Carina moved down the aisle, piling the needed items in the basket. The woman continued to watch her, making her nerves jump.

"Then what are you doing with Brock's kid and shopping for their usual supplies?" The woman was sure inquisitive. Coming from the city Carina learned you didn't tell strangers anything about yourself. They could be looking for a way to rob, rape, or murder you. She was sure this woman wasn't looking to do anything more than stab her in the back with false accusations, and she wasn't about to hand her the knife.

"I guess you'll have to ask Brock." Carina pushed the cart up the candy aisle. She snagged a bag of M&Ms for each of the kids.

The door opened as the woman said, "I still say he picked you up in a bar."

"I did not pick *Ms. Valencia* up in a bar," Brock's voice boomed across the store. The woman jumped and blushed before hurrying back to her spot at the counter.

Relief oozed out of Carina in a long breath.

"She's a nanny and is staying with us to teach Maddie and take care of Tate." The authority in Brock's voice made her smile. She watched him stride up the aisle toward her. Taking Tate from the cart, he nodded for her to push it to the counter.

The woman took a defiant stance. "How am I supposed to believe you're paying a nanny when you can barely afford these groceries?"

"I believe that is my business and not yours. Total these." His voice was hard as steel. He watched the woman punch the price of each item into an old cash register.

Brock stared at the candy and then at Carina. "Is that a necessity?"

"I believe it is." She looked him straight in the eye.

"For you or the kids?"

She glared at him. "The kids."

"I'll not have you spoiling them."

"One bag of candy isn't going to spoil them. If it bothers you that much, I'll pay for them." She grabbed the candy out of the cart and reached into her pocket for the ten-dollar bill she'd stuffed there before leaving the house.

"You don't have to do that." He grabbed the candy back, tossing it in the cart.

"I'll use my own money to spoil the children." She grabbed them back.

"You sure you two aren't shacking up?" the woman asked.

Carina glared at the woman at the same time as Brock.

"She's the nanny."

"I'm the nanny." They said simultaneously.

"Put the candy on the counter," Brock ordered. "The phones aren't working here either, so you'll have to go to the hill south of town." His tone and hard eyes made her drop the candy and head for the door.

At the door, she pivoted and glared at him. "Which way is south?"

"Left."

She held her temper long enough to not slam the door, but she turned left and stalked down the road.

He was so pig-headed. How could he think one bag of candy would spoil his kids? She huffed and grumbled about the man all the way to the top of the hill.

Looking out across the expanse of sage, tufts of light green grass, and sandy soil, she took a deep breath. The tang of sage mixed with the fresh air settled her anger. The spectacular scene with the mountains making a jagged backdrop in the distance captured her admiration. It wasn't the lush pictures she'd seen of Oregon on calendars, but it wasn't butt ugly. She liked the gnarly looking bushes and small rises waving with tufts of grass.

Pulling her cell phone out of her pocket, she turned it on. Spinning in a circle, she stopped when it showed full reception. She quickly dialed Georgie's number, hoping her friend was home.

"Yo."

Carina fell silent. Who was answering Georgie's phone?

"Hello?" the male voice said, again.

"Is Georgie there?" Carina asked, wondering if this was her friend's newest live-in. She'd yet to meet Georgie's latest love of her life.

"Yeah." She held the phone away from her ear as he hollered, "It's for you!"

"Well, who is it?" Georgie yelled back.

"Who are you?" he asked.

"Tell her a far-away friend," she said, knowing it would get Georgie's curiosity going.

"A far-away—" he didn't finish the sentence before Georgie shrieked and breathed into the phone.

"I haven't heard from you since we were cut off." Georgie blurted. "And I've tried to call you on the cell and it would never go through."

It was so good to hear her friend's voice, tears burned in Carina's eyes. "There was a major storm that night. We lost power and phone service."

"How's it going? Have you figured out how to stay longer?"

"Brock offered to sell some of his antiques to keep me a few more months." *He wants me to stay*. Her heart pattered in her chest.

"That's good. You need more time away from here." Georgie lowered her voice. "Your mom's been over several times wanting to know how to contact you."

Carina felt small for not leaving any information with her mother, but she needed the space for just a little while longer. "When I'm ready to talk to her, I'll give her a call."

"Perry was asking about you the other day." The contempt in Georgie's voice was palpable.

Hair on the back of Carina's neck prickled. "What does he care? He stopped caring what I did long before I lost our child."

"He said something about some papers to sign."

"The divorce is final. What more needs signed?" As far as she knew everything was taken care of. The house was sold and the money split. She'd put her half in an investment since as a nanny she wasn't in need of a place to live.

She sighed. "I'll give him a call and see what he wants."

"I wouldn't. Let him fret it out. You've moved on and he needs to let you." Georgie had never been an advocate for Perry, but she'd tolerated him at gatherings.

Carina looked back toward Dutch Springs, then turned back toward the cell tower. "I think I'm going to have trouble leaving here."

"It's a good thing Brock thought of a way to keep you." The chuckle in her friend's voice sent her senses on alert.

"What do you mean?"

"The longer you stay the better he gets to know you, and who knows—" she let the rest hang in the air.

"I can't even think like that! I have to keep my heart and feelings toward this family neutral."

"Yeah, I can see you're doing that well!" The laughter on the other end of the phone upset her.

She'd enjoyed Brock's embrace. Her heart had gone out to both the children. She was in deep trouble. She'd broken all the rules she vowed wouldn't happen.

"What's he like?"

"Who?"

"The father. "

"Georgie, I'm in trouble." Brock's bare pecs and eyes blazing with desire flashed before her.

"What do you mean?"

"He's gorgeous, and I'm drawn to him stronger than any man I've ever met before. And it scares me."

Georgie laughed. "Who are you teaching the kids or the father?"

"It isn't funny, Georgie! He's more masculine than any man I've encountered in my life. He's strong, yet so gentle and caring with his children."

"So, what's the problem? You're single, he's single…"

"I don't have plans for a man in my life."

"Who says he'll be in your life? Have some fun and when you move on, you move on."

The casual way Georgie could move in and out of relationships had always confused Carina.

"You know I can't do that."

"You can't spend the rest of your life being a nun," Georgie's voice shook with aversion.

"Brock doesn't want to get tangled up with a woman again. He's been married twice. His first wife died." She stopped and thought. "I haven't figured out what happened, but he still loves her. Then he remarried, hoping for a mother for his daughter and that woman birthed a beautiful, little boy and left. Shattering all of them." She shook her head. "The father and daughter are close."

"But they both like you. Everyone likes you. Do the nanny thing, crawl in his bed, and have fun. If he isn't looking for a long-term thing then you're in the clear. When it's over come home."

Carina shook her head. Georgie was a dear friend, but she never understood Carina's need for a family. "I'm not sure when I'll get to call you. They haven't any idea when the phone lines will be repaired. But when they are I'll call, I promise."

"Take care."

"I will and you do the same. Tell my mom I'm fine—and I miss her."

"I will."

"Bye, Georgie."

"Bye."

Carina flipped her phone closed and debated whether to call her mom. She missed her mother's absentmindedness. No, she still wasn't ready to deal with her mother. As much as she loved the woman, her interfering and neediness Carina couldn't deal with yet.

Sluggish steps carried her back to the cluster of buildings. She'd left everything behind her to try and make a new start. So far, she'd kept all her guilt and loss hidden from Brock. But would taking Brock up on his offer and staying longer be a mistake?

If she stayed longer, would she be able to walk away from the family? She couldn't take a loss like that again so soon. The pieces wouldn't be easy to pick up and put back together.

She stopped, spun away from Dutch Springs, and stared across the vast stretch of land. A person could get used to seeing only land and sky and the whisper of the wind carrying the far-off call of a bird.

But she was a city girl. And though staying longer in these beautiful surroundings appealed to her, the thought of more time around Brock frightened her.

Eight

Sitting in the small restaurant, Carina felt the eyes of every one of Rayanne's family members on her. The three other tables had at least three people sitting at them. She tried to stare out the dusty window, fringed with a smoke-stained curtain which had once been yellow with colorful flowers. A loud laugh from the counter brought her attention to the men seated on the seven bar stools. The place was packed and according to Maddie, they were all locals.

"Why is everyone staring?" she whispered across the table to Brock.

"They always do that when someone new shows up." He bit his hamburger and winked at Maddie.

"Even if someone passing through stops for a burger?" Having so many eyes watch her eat curbed her appetite. It also reminded her of Perry. He'd watched her every move before the miscarriage. Almost as if he expected her to do something to thwart the child's arrival. Guilt washed through her like a shot of cold air. Did he realize she would do something to harm their child? Was that why he grew so distant and cold after the miscarriage? He blamed her as much as she blamed herself? Carina shivered and glanced down at the smashed burger bun. She'd lost her appetite.

"I told them you were a nanny."

Carina peeked at Maddie, pulling her out of her agony-filled thoughts.

"They've never seen any except the one who talks funny on TV." Maddie poked a fry in her mouth and handed one to Tate.

"Oh, wonderful! They think I'm a television personality?"

"No. I told them you were a plain, old teacher." Maddie grinned.

Brock added, "They don't see too many teachers without gray hair and wrinkles around here. Most of our teachers are retired from other areas and end up being asked to teach. In case you hadn't noticed, not too many people live around here. You just about have to grow up here to like the isolation and the barren countryside."

"Oh, but I thought the view from the hill where I called Georgie was breathtaking!" It stunned her to think people would find the area barren. "I watched a bunny hop from bush to bush and there was something tan, white, and black moving farther out."

"That would be antelope." Brock rubbed a fry around in the ketchup in his basket.

"Really? I've never seen one up close. Are there any at Haven?" Carina wanted to see all the local flora and fauna while she worked at the ranch.

"If you ride out among the cattle and the high sage." The guarded look in his eyes made her smile. He knew where that statement would lead.

"When will you start my riding lessons so I can see some antelope?" she asked, flashing him a challenging smile.

His jaw clenched, and she knew the answer.

"I said you weren't going to ride horses here," he answered in a low growl.

"Why don't you want the others to know what we're talking about? Or don't you want them to see us arguing?" she added when Brock flinched and scanned the tables closest to them.

She raised a brow and looked at Maddie. The child ignored them as she stuffed fries into Tate's little fists.

"Both. Are you finished? We should head back." He tossed his napkin in the red basket.

Carina tucked her leftover fries in a napkin along with her half-eaten burger. She'd finish her meal later—away from everyone's curious stares.

"Come on Maddie, let's take Tate to the truck while your dad pays the bill."

The woman Maddie had pointed out as Rayanne's mother hurried across the room. "Was everything to your satisfaction, Ms. Valencia?" she asked, wiping her hands on her apron.

"It was fine. I'm just not very hungry." Carina felt bad that the woman saw her put the food in a napkin.

"If you stay in these parts just being outside will give you an appetite."

She smiled at the woman. "I'm hoping to see more of this area, hopefully, by horseback."

"Oh, Maddie's the one to take you. She's a good a horsewoman just like her mother."

A troubled expression crossed the woman's face leading Carina to wonder about Beth.

"I hope we see you again soon." The woman ruffled the hair on Maddie's head. "And you young lady. Rayanne doesn't get to see you enough."

Maddie glanced up at Carina. "Hopefully with a nanny, I can come see her more." The wistfulness in the child's voice tugged at Carina.

"We'll see what can be managed." Carina tucked Tate on her hip and headed out the door with Maddie skipping behind, shouting her goodbyes to everyone.

Brock watched them leave. He never thought a woman herding his kids around would lighten his heart, but watching the way Carina handled his children did.

"Why are you smilin'?" Rayanne's uncle asked, taking a seat at the table and eating fries left on Maddie's plate.

Brock cringed and glared at the scraggly bearded man. "Just thinking about how good it's going to feel getting that damn banker paid off."

"Well, we's got us a bet that you're paying that there pretty nanny in bed privilege—"

Brock had a hold of Stan's collar before he could finish his thought. He yanked the man up and shook him.

"If I hear any rumors like that, you better be hiding." He'd never really liked the man, even when they attended school together. He tightened the collar enough Stan's face reddened. "Ms. Valencia is here to take care of my kids and that's all."

"She's awful good looking to only be watching after kids," one of the other men in the room said and snickered. "She lookin' for a man? I'd keep her happy."

Brock shoved Stan away from him and stood in the center of the restaurant. How could these men even have such thoughts about a woman they didn't know? One who had shown herself as nothing but respectable the whole time she'd been in Dutch Springs.

Someone had turned their bias against Carina. He smashed his cap on his head. There was only one person who would benefit most by Carina tucking tail and leaving. His ex-father-in-law.

He scanned the room, making eye contact with each male in the establishment. "If any of you make a pass or lay a hand on her, or if any of your women wag vicious tongues about Ms. Valencia—you're liable to have a cattle stampede through your quaint, little community."

With his threat hanging in the air, Brock left the building.

The nerve of these people thinking things were anything other than appropriate. There were children in the house for crying out loud. And probably the exact forum his ex-father-in-law would use to get custody of Maddie. He stomped out to the pickup. Tate was already asleep in the car seat while Maddie leaned against Carina with her eyes closed.

Brock took a deep breath to calm his anger before opening the door and sliding in.

"What took so long?" Carina asked quietly, peering at him over the sleeping children.

"A couple of the men asked about the road between here and Haven." Lying had never been something Brock stomached, but he damn sure wasn't going to tell Carina how the people of Dutch Springs speculated on her wages. It still rankled they'd jump to such conclusions without even meeting the woman. Never mind the last woman connected with him had come from a bar and hadn't made any friends among the community.

"I hope I don't have to come back here again soon." She leaned her head against the back of the seat.

"Why?"

"I didn't like the way they all stared at me like I escaped from the zoo." She shuddered and closed her eyes.

"They don't mean anything. They just don't have a whole lot of excitement around here." He started the pickup.

"Some of their looks weren't inquisitive. They were hostile."

"No one's going to hurt you. I promise."

She tilted her head toward him and opened her eyes. The late afternoon sun glittered in the tears welling in her eyes. "You don't need to protect me." Her words were whispered. The waver in her voice reminded him of the young men he fought beside in the Gulf. She was afraid. But he didn't think the locals caused her tears.

"How about you tell me about the big city to keep me alert on the drive back?" he offered, hoping to take her mind off whatever made her sad.

"What do you want to know?"

He backed the pickup away from the curb and headed toward Haven. "Everything. I've never been to a big city."

"Never? What about when you were in the service?"

His head jerked around so fast, his neck popped. "How do you know I was in the service?"

"Your background check." She sighed. "And some

letters I found in the bottom of the Grandfather clock."

"What letters?"

"You didn't know they were there?" She shifted, sitting straighter and turning toward him the best she could with Maddie using her for a pillow.

"No." He scratched his head. What letters could she be talking about? His mom wouldn't have kept the letters he wrote. She wasn't sentimental. *Beth*. But he thought he'd thrown them all out after…

"Ones you wrote to Beth while you were overseas. By the date, I'd say you were in Desert Storm?"

"Yeah." He stared at the road ahead. "It's not something I like to remember."

"I'm not bringing it up to bring back bad memories. Your letters told me a lot about Beth. But not enough to get a clear picture of her."

"I asked you about the big city, how are we on the subject of my wife?" He growled out the sentence and stared ahead. His fingers ached as his hands fisted around the steering wheel. He didn't want to talk about her. It hurt too much.

"Sorry."

She plucked at the back of the seat with nervous fingers. He glanced over. Indecision wrinkled her brow.

"I just wanted to know what kind of woman could keep a man's heart locked up even after she's gone." Her soft words roared in his ears.

His heart beat faster thinking of Beth. She was the fresh air after a storm, the sweetness of rain, and the gentleness of an evening breeze. He glanced at the woman watching him. She was the storm. His heart went from the patter of loss to the thud of desire. Where Beth had soothed his young brashness, this woman fired him up.

Pulling his gaze back to the road, he pondered his newfound knowledge as Carina launched into a description of Chicago he could have read out of a book.

His eyelids grew heavy when her voice penetrated the zone he'd gone into. "So, why doesn't Beth's parents help with Maddie?"

The anger he'd stuffed into a dark hole in his heart consumed him. He didn't even glance down to make sure Maddie slept before saying. "Because her father is an asshole."

His grip on the steering wheel tightened as he relived the day in the hospital when Beth was taken off life support. His gut twisted and rage made his head throb as if it would explode.

It took all Carina's resolve to not shrink against the door when the anger in Brock filled the cab of the truck. She glanced over her shoulder to Tate sleeping in the car seat, then down at Maddie. She didn't want either of them to wake while their father was in this state.

Cautiously, she opened her mouth and asked, "Why—" Brock looked at her, his mouth set in a hard line even, his eyes dulled with pain. She cleared her throat. "Why do you say that?"

"Maxwell Johnson always wanted someone more for his daughter. Someone not of this land. Someone who could cover her in diamonds." His hands squeezed the wheel, and he turned jerkily around a bend in the road. "I wasn't his top pick for a husband. We kept our love secret from Beth's father for many years. But when he found out, Beth had to leave home. Johnson was a violent man when things didn't go his way. How her sweet mother put up with it all those years I'll never know."

Brock's eyes turned steely and his mouth twisted in a sardonic smile. "The day we took Beth off life support," Brock swallowed, tears glistening in his eyes, "Johnson had the balls to say she was better off dead than as my wife." Brock stared at her over the head of his beautiful daughter. "She was better off dead than being *my* wife." The anguish on his face made her heart ache for him. She reached out touching his arm.

"He was in pain, too. Most likely he didn't mean what he said."

Brock shook off her hand. "No. He meant it. I neglected her. I didn't ride with her that day and her horse fell. By the time I realized she hadn't returned and found her…" He jerked the pickup to a stop and leaned over the steering wheel. His body heaved as he sobbed.

Carina shuffled Maddie, careful not to wake her, until she could sit next to Brock. Not knowing how he'd react, she cautiously placed her hand on his back. When he didn't try to shake her off, she made large slow circles. Giving him the human contact she sensed he needed.

All these years, he'd blamed himself for his wife's death.

It was an unfortunate accident. His father-in-law's words had to have hindered the healing process.

Maddie squirmed in the seat and raised her head. "What's wrong with Daddy?" she asked, glancing from her father to Carina.

"He's tired." Carina continued to rub his back. "Go back to sleep. When he's had a rest, we'll head home."

Carina smiled at the child to reassure her. Maddie didn't need to learn about the callousness of her grandparent nor the hatred her father held for the man.

Maddie leaned back against the locked door but didn't quite close her eyes. Carina chuckled to herself. The girl was protective of her father.

Brock shifted his head, his teary gaze meeting Carina's. Apprehension lingered in his eyes. She smiled and continued rubbing his back. She wasn't ready to relinquish the contact between them.

"Did you have a good rest?" she asked, motioning with her head toward Maddie who hadn't fallen back to sleep, though she tried hard to make it appear so.

Brock peered around her to see his daughter and cleared his throat. "Yeah." He cleared his throat again and squeezed her arm. "I had a good rest."

He leaned toward her and whispered. "Thank you." His warm breath fluttered her hair and sent shivers of elation dancing through her body.

"You're welcome." She stared forward when he started the truck. The heat and strength of his solid body next to hers took all her resolve to not snuggle closer. Brock dropped his hand onto her leg. She glanced his way and he smiled, giving her knee a squeeze like they'd rode next to each other before and his hand upon her wasn't anything out of the ordinary.

Her heart pounding in her chest said otherwise.

Nine

Carina carried Tate up to his bed while Brock deposited Maddie in hers. They met at the top of the stairs.

"You want some hot chocolate or something to eat?" she asked, heading down the stairs in front of him. Carina wanted to stay aloof from the man. She couldn't have a relationship with anyone until she let go of the guilt, but she wasn't ready for the night to end.

"Do you have any cookies to go with the hot chocolate?" he asked.

She glanced over her shoulder and smiled. "Yes. Chocolate chip." The grin he bestowed upon her sent her nerves tingling. Carina hurried down the hall and into the kitchen to start the water boiling. It had taken her a while to get used to not using a microwave for everything. This house contained only necessary appliances.

Brock sat down at the table and watched her move about the room. His gaze followed her every move and reminded her of the men at the restaurant.

"Please don't watch me," she said, facing him and staring square in his face.

He looked taken aback. "Why?"

"It reminds me of the men back at the restaurant. I've been in all types of neighborhoods in Chicago, but I've never run into a room full of people that made me that nervous."

"Sorry. It's been a while since I wanted to watch a woman in my kitchen."

His words warmed and saddened her. She wanted him to accept her, but when the month was up, she had to head back to Chicago whether she was emotionally healed or not. To stay any longer would make leaving all the more difficult.

"I didn't mean to make you sad." He reached out to her.

She wanted to put her hand in his, but she couldn't. Not if she wanted to eventually walk away.

"It's not you." Placing the two cups of hot chocolate on the table, she sat down across from him. Staring into his eyes, she saw he didn't believe her. But that was just as well. Let him think she wasn't attracted to him. It was best.

She cleared her throat determined to find a way to get him help when she left. "I don't want to stir up old wounds, but where are Beth's parents now? Couldn't her mother help out with the kids?"

Anger returned to his eyes like bolts of lightning. "Her mother passed away a year ago. Her father kept the ranch, but has someone else running it while he works for the bank in Halverton." He ground his teeth as his gaze swept the room. "He's the one hoping I fail to pay off the mortgage this year. Ever since Evelyn passed, he's been trying his damnedest to wreck me and get custody of Maddie."

"What about you and Tate? Not to mention what it would do to Maddie to take her from you." Carina couldn't believe a man could be so low. Why torture his own family this way?

"He hadn't spoken with or cared a lick about Maddie until his wife died. Since losing both his women all he rants about is getting Maddie and giving her a better life than I can." Brock stared at her; his eyes full of sorrow. "If it hadn't been for Maddie when Beth died, I could have easily become resentful like Maxwell."

"I don't believe that." Carina reached across the table, grabbing his hand. "You're a good man who loves deeply and cares about the right things. It sounds to me like Mr. Johnson was already a bitter man before Beth's death."

Gazing into his eyes and holding his hand, Carina's body roused from compassion to passion. Her nipples tingled and her body warmed. She had to get away.

Now.

"It's late." She dropped his hand and stood, screeching the chair backward in her haste.

Brock stared at her, his eyes full of questions.

"You didn't do anything. I just…need to get some sleep." She walked to the doorway and turned. "Good night."

Hurrying up the stairs, her heart thudded in her chest, not from the exertion, but the thoughts dancing in her head. If he had made the move, she would have been in his arms and possibly sprawled across the table before either of them thought of the consequences.

***

Brock sat at the table. What did he do to make her take off like a scared jackrabbit? He played the conversation over in his mind. She grasped his hand. He smiled. Her hand was long and thin. Many times over the last few days, he'd wondered what those fingers would feel like running through his hair and trailing across his skin.

The kitchen grew warm. He placed the mugs in the sink and turned off the light. With Jack back and Carina here to watch the kids, he could get a lot more accomplished in a day.

He started up the stairs, but his mind ran through the list of chores for the next day, and he didn't feel a bit sleepy. Detouring, he went into his office, plopped into his desk chair, and pulled out a notepad. He scribbled all the things that needed done. Then he listed them in the most effective order.

Finishing the list, he took it down the hall and set it on the kitchen counter. Moving through the dark house was second nature to him. He'd grown up here and furniture never got moved except for a yearly cleaning underneath. He climbed the stairs knowing which one would creak.

Smiling, he slid his hand along the handrail. Maddie had the same love of the land and the house as he and Beth. She may go away to college, but she'd be back. The high desert was too much a part of her. That was if he could keep her out of Maxwell's hands.

"No! Please…no!" Carina's whimpering stood his hair on end.

Brock sprinted up the stairs and around the banister to Carina's door.

"No! Please, don't take her!" Her voice went from hysteria to whimpering.

He didn't even bother knocking. The sounds coming from the room tore at his heart. Turning the knob, he burst into the room. It was dark, but he'd been wandering around in the dark a while and his eyes focused just fine. Carina lay curled in a fetal position against the headboard. Her frightened whimper pierced his heart and sent him across the room to gather her in his arms.

She shoved him, crying out, "No! You can't have her!" She clawed at him, her nails raking his neck.

"Carina, it's me, Brock." He reached out, clicking on the lamp beside the bed before wrapping his arms around her. When she tried to get away, he hugged her gently, but firmly. "Shhh. I won't hurt you. You're dreaming." Grasping her shoulders, he shook her gently. "Carina, wake up."

Her eyelids slowly rose. Sorrow lit her eyes until she became fully awake. She lunged at him, hugging him around the neck, and sobbed.

Brock held her, stroking her back. The feel of the satin material under his hands sent heat to his groin. Feeling her curves, after so many days of wondering about them, had his body rigid and wanting.

"You're fine. No one's hurting you. I wouldn't let them. Shhh. There now." When she stopped shaking, he gently held her away from him. His breath caught at the sight of her alabaster skin against the dark, shiny material of a skimpy nightie.

"What was that all about?" he asked, pushing her thick, dark hair out of her face. The softness and weight of her tresses made his fingers itch to do more than gently tuck it behind her ear.

"I have bad dreams." She wouldn't look him in the eye.

"Was it something you ate?" He smiled, trying to make light of the dream.

She shook her head but didn't respond to the humor.

"Is there anything I can do?"

The flicker of distress in her eyes and the softly whispered, "No one can help me," was the highest form of torture he'd ever endured. Was the reality of her dreams why she'd taken a job so far from her family and friends? What in her life could have been so horrendous to plague her dreams? Not her divorce.

He pulled Carina into his arms. She didn't fight him. Her body flowed against his like molasses over oats. Even knowing she was tormented by her past, he couldn't stop the desire that flared in him.

He slipped a finger under her chin, lifting her face to gaze into her eyes. Sorrow no longer glistened in their blue depth. Desire burned.

Without thinking of consequences other than wanting to taste her lips, he lowered his head. Her breath was warm and sweet. She kissed him with abandon. The rush of heat and emotion storming his body made him lightheaded.

Carina was fully awake now. The dream had drained her, grief stole her strength. As Brock plied her with warm, passion-filled kisses, her body became energized and sizzled for more. She ran her hands up his firm chest, moving to circle his neck.

Something warm and sticky touched her fingers. She pulled back, glancing down at her hand. "What's this?" she asked.

He held her hand and studied it. "It looks like blood."

"On your neck?"

He raised a hand, touching the bleeding scratches. "Yeah."

When he didn't offer to say more, she prodded. "How did you scratch your neck?"

He watched her a minute, then took her hands. "You did it."

"Me?" Why—how would she scratch him? They'd only been kissing and her hands hadn't been near his neck until just now.

"During your dream. I tried to wake you. You fought like a wildcat at first, scratching and flailing."

Mortified, she raised up on her knees, capturing his head in her hands. "Brock, I'm so sorry." She'd never been a violent person. Not until losing her child. In her dreams she fought with every inch of her being to keep the child. Now she knew why she woke emotionally and physically drained. "Let me take care of it." She started to scoot off the bed, but he grabbed her around the middle, dragging her back.

"It's only a scratch and you didn't know what you were doing. I forgive you." He nuzzled her neck, sending waves of heat out to her toes. Her body shouted 'give in', while her conscience knew better.

"I think you should go now." She kissed him to reduce the abruptness of her change of heart. "The kids. It isn't…"

Brock slid a hand up under her night slip, lightly resting it high on her thigh.

"No, it isn't proper. You're right." He captured her

mouth with his, stealing her breath away and leaving her sprawled across the bed.

He backed away smiling, his eyes shining with devilment. Before she could think of anything to say, he disappeared out the door.

Brock closed the door quietly and started down the hall to his room. If she hadn't remained sane, he would have—

"Daddy."

Startled, he spun about. Maddie stood in her doorway framed by the soft glow of her bed lamp.

"What are you doing up at this hour?" he asked, changing direction and heading toward her.

"I heard a woman crying. It scared me. When I came to get you, I saw you go in Carina's room." Her young eyes didn't accuse. But he felt like a lowlife. His daughter shouldn't see him go in and come out of the woman's room, especially after Carina's words.

"Carina had a nightmare. I went in and woke her up, and talked to her a while so she could go back to sleep."

"Why is your neck bleeding?"

Brock put a hand on his neck where Carina had scratched him. "I told you she had a nightmare. She fought me at first thinking I attacked her, I guess."

"But you'd never hurt her," Maddie admonished, coming to his defense.

"Carina knows that. She was still asleep. Once she woke up and realized it was me, she calmed down." He wrapped his arms around his daughter. "Don't say anything in the morning. I have a feeling she's going to be embarrassed."

"I wouldn't do anything to make Carina feel bad."

The sincerity in her young voice made his heart skip.

"I know you wouldn't. Go to bed Freckles. I have a big day planned tomorrow, and I'll need your help."

She tugged on his sleeve as had become their ritual. He bent down so she could kiss his cheek. "I love you, Daddy."

"I know you do, Freckles, and I love you and Tate." He kissed her cheek and gave her one last hug before sending her off to bed.

Not only did he have a ranch to run, but he also wished to find out more about their nanny. He'd believed all along she hid from something. After tonight, he knew she was hurting from something. The sorrow and torture in her eyes told him it was more than a divorce.

His groin ached and throbbed, reliving Carina in his arms. Her slinky nightie under his hands while learning her curves and the satiny skin of her thigh would haunt him. Her vulnerability had frayed the edges of his resistance.

His attraction to her had to do with their proximity and her vulnerability. He refused to think he needed her for anything more than helping with his children. From here on out, he'd keep his hands to himself and their relationship platonic. It was the only way he could keep his family together—and his heart intact.

Ten

Brock stumbled down the stairs, his head groggy and his mouth dry as a dust storm. After going to bed, he'd thought about Carina's dreams. Trying to rationalize what could bring her such sorrow and vicious defending. The only thing he could think of was rape. Had she been raped? It would account for the dreams and the way she attacked him, but she said something about 'don't take her'.

All the scenarios that bounced in his head had given him nightmares of his own, reliving the horrors he'd witnessed in the war.

He needed coffee. *Strong coffee.*

In the kitchen, he filled the pot with water and switched the coffeemaker on. He dumped double the usual amount of grounds in the filter and stared out the window. A pink glow bloomed over the barn roof, highlighting the surroundings in a fresh blush. The pink slowly turned gold then yellow as the sun rose in the sky. A slight frost dusted the pickup. Winter was coming.

"Good morning." Carina's soft, raspy morning voice ignited the embers from the night before. The ones he'd told himself not to heed.

He slowly turned half hoping she'd still be in the flimsy nightie. Seeing her in jeans and a form-hugging T-shirt didn't squelch the need building in him. *Damn!* How was he to think of her as his children's nanny when one glance had his body craving to take her?

"Morning."

Carina smiled bashfully and moved by him to the coffee pot. She filled a mug and handed it to him. "You look like you need this more than me."

"Thanks," he said sarcastically and sat at the table. "Oh!"

At her exclamation, he glanced over his shoulder. She stood on her tiptoes staring out the kitchen window. Her firm rounded bottom begged to be handled. He slid from the chair, moving behind her.

"Oh, what?" he asked, placing his hands on her shoulders, when he really wanted to cup her bottom.

"That's the most beautiful sunrise I think I've ever seen." She tipped her head back to rest against his shoulder. The feel of her body and her acceptance of his touch spun all the reasons he quoted himself during the night to stay aloof out of his head. He wanted to spend many mornings just this way, with Carina in his arms watching the sunrise.

"Stick around, you'll see many more." The words were out before he could rein them back.

She turned in his arms. "This is only a temporary position. You haven't the funds to keep me on. And Tate will soon be old enough to go with you every day." The sadness in her eyes reflected the ache in his heart.

He'd known she wasn't staying. He wanted that. *Really*.

He dropped his arms from their perch on her shoulders and walked into the mudroom to put on his boots and get the day started.

"Where are you going?" she asked, standing in the doorway, uncertainty flickering in her eyes.

"I've got cows to check. I'll be back in an hour and a half for breakfast. Tell Maddie I'll need her help this morning."

"Ok." Carina watched Brock put on his hat and coat and hurry out the door. She stood in the doorway listening to his boots crunch across the frozen grass and the truck start up. They became closer last night, and though her heart swelled at the memory, she knew it couldn't be. Until she came to grips with the fact she failed to bring a child into this world, she couldn't find peace with herself or anyone else.

"Wow! You beat me up this morning!" Maddie skipped into the kitchen.

"Yes, I did. Not bad for a city slicker." She tweaked the girl's nose and began pulling out the fry pans.

"Did you make the coffee or Daddy?"

"Your father. He left to check the cows and said he'd be back in an hour and a half." She turned back around. "How…" Maddie watched her with a strange look on her face. "Did I do something wrong?" she asked.

"No." Maddie opened the refrigerator door.

"You were looking at me funny. You sure I didn't do something to upset you?" Did Maddie see her father come out of her room last night? Dear God, how did she explain that to a pre-teen? She'd think the worst when it had all be so innocent. Her body warmed, remembering the shared kisses. Well, mostly innocent.

"No. I just…Daddy said not to embarrass you, but I can't figure out what a grownup would have nightmares about." Maddie poured milk into a glass and returned the milk jug to the refrigerator. Her actions gave Carina time to decide what to say.

"Grownups have fears just like kids. Only ours usually have to do with things on our minds. Sometimes when there are so many they all bunch together and it's like they attack us. They do it in our sleep when we're more vulnerable." She watched Maddie. "Does that make sense?"

"Kind of. But if it's just things, why did you attack Daddy?"

Carina's stomach twisted and her heart raced. *Because I thought he was the person taking my baby.*

"In my dream, I was fighting someone. When your father tried to wake me, I continued to fight."

Maddie was a perceptive girl. She didn't know how much longer she could keep her secret from both the girl and her father. But she had to. She had to reconcile with herself before she could move into any relationship. This family was only a stepping stone to get to where she wanted to be in life.

At the thought of leaving them, her chest squeezed. How could she leave this family in three weeks? They had all taken a spot in her heart.

***

Brock bounced down the county road as fast as he could without flying over the bumps and landing in the

122

bar pit. Roscoe sat on the seat next to him staring intently out the window as if they chased something rather than Brock running away from the nanny and how she made him feel.

After telling Carina he was checking cattle, he decided to have a talk with Willie T. If he hurried, he'd catch the old man at Dutch Springs restaurant for his daily dose of caffeine. The back road was cleared now and it only took him half an hour to get there.

Sure enough, Willie T's battered, but smooth-running, old pickup sat in front of the restaurant. Brock parked alongside the rusty vehicle and hurried into the building.

"You look a little worse for wear," Rayanne's dad, Charlie said, getting up from the counter next to Willie T. "You been overpaying that nanny?"

Brock glared at the man's remark and started toward him. Willie T put out a hand and looked at Charlie.

"If you are talking about the nice lady who is taking care of Brock's kids, then I think you have some apologizing to do to both Brock and the lady." Willie T stood up. "And if this is the kind of talk that is going around about the nice lady—I'll have to drink my morning coffee elsewhere." He took Brock by the arm and led him toward the door.

"B-but Willie T, you've been drinking coffee here for twenty years," Charlie called.

"I guess it's time for a change."

Brock pushed open the door. He cherished Willie T as much as he had his father and after that show of support for both he and Carina, he valued the man even more.

"Thanks, Willie T," he said as they leaned on the hood of his pickup.

"You don't have to thank me, I only said the truth. That lady isn't what everyone around here is thinking and saying." He nodded his head as though he'd just uttered a decree. "You thought of calling up Maxwell and telling him to lay off the shit he's been slinging?"

"I doubt if it will help." Brock scowled. "He's got more money and clout around here than I do."

"But not as much integrity." Willie T slapped him on the back.

"Thanks. But right now, that isn't getting the bank or Maxwell off my back. It also isn't keeping folks from thinking what they're thinking."

"How's the nanny working out?" Willie T asked, rubbing his hand back and forth across the rusty hood of his pickup.

"She had a nightmare last night that left her emotionally and physically drained."

Willie T stood back, glaring at him. "You aren't doing what all these people have been saying are you?"

"No! God no! There are kids in the house. You know me better than that."

"Good. For a minute there I thought you were sleeping with the woman, although, it would do you both good." Willie T grinned from ear to ear, showing his tobacco-stained teeth.

"That it would. But I can't allow my body to overrule my head. It would be the worst thing I could do for either of us to let things go that far."

"Why?"

"She's only here for a month unless I figure out how to pay for her services. God knows Maddie's load has been lightened and Tate loves her." His lower regions flared as he thought of Carina carrying Tate on her hip. Thoughts like that only got him deeper into an area he didn't want to go. "And she's what I need to keep the social services and Maxwell at bay."

"So figure out a way to keep her. Don't you have anything you can sell?" Willie rubbed his calloused hands together. The scratchy sound reminded Brock of the old phonograph sitting in the corner of his office.

"Yeah, I can think of a couple of antiques I could sell."

"Then do it."

Brock smiled. *Yeah. Do it*. He was pretty sure Carina would have some ideas of how to sell the family heirlooms. There were a few of them that meant as much to him as his children and land.

"So why was Carina having dreams?" Willie's direct question threw Brock back into the mood he'd been in when he pulled up to the restaurant.

"I'm not sure. I think it's the reason she hired on as a nanny so far from everything and everyone she knows."

"Think it's a man?" Willie T's direct question squeezed Brock's stomach with jealousy. Was she dreaming about her husband leaving? Had that upset her more than she let on? He didn't think so. She seemed more bitter than broke up over the divorce.

"I don't think it's that. She said her marriage broke up over her health." He looked at Willie T. "What kind of a man would divorce a woman with health issues?"

"Not a decent one. She looks healthy though a bit skinny to me."

"Yeah, that's what I was thinking." He looked up

at the man who seemed to know a person's makeup with one meeting. "Do you think it was a mental problem?" If so, his children could be in danger.

"Not, like that. I saw much grief and sorrow in her, but not craziness." Willie T peered out across the sagebrush-dotted terrain. "I think she needs time and compassion."

"If she can help me sell the old furniture around the house, she'll have time. And as long as she treats my kids respectfully, she'll have my compassion."

"Give her time to get to trust you, and I'm sure you will learn all you want from the woman." The old man pulled a pouch of tobacco out of his pocket.

"How can you be so certain?"

"I have been around a long time and watched people." Willie T smiled, slipping a pinch of tobacco into his cheek.

"Do you think you know more than the people who have degrees in Psychology?" Brock studied the man. He always wondered how the old man knew so much about everything and everyone.

Willie T scratched his head and shrugged. "Now, where am I going to go for coffee every morning since I told Charlie I won't be coming in there?" He jerked his thumb toward the restaurant.

"Don't you own a coffeemaker? It would be cheaper."

"I like conversation with my coffee. There's no one at my house for conversation. And my kids don't like me coming over more than once a week."

"You could visit us once a week. That would only leave you one day to drink your coffee alone," Brock offered.

"Deal. I'll follow you home."

Brock climbed into his pickup and hoped Willie T didn't start interrogating Carina the minute he set foot in the house.

***

Carina didn't know how to act around Brock when he came back. They had bridged one gap in their relationship, which made more problems than it solved. She wanted him to hold her, but at the same time, she couldn't allow herself the attachment. Just thinking of leaving tore her up inside.

"Carina? Carina, Tate's been crying for a while now." Maddie stared at her from across the kitchen where she flipped pancakes.

"Oh, I'm sorry. I guess I didn't sleep that well after my…you know." Carina tossed the dishrag into the sink and hurried upstairs to get Tate dressed and ready for the day. Entering the room, her heart fluttered. The child smiled through big crocodile tears trickling down his rosy cheeks. He held his arms wide. She picked him up and hugged him tight.

Inhaling his baby scent and holding him close, tears burned in her eyes. Taking the position of a nanny she never dreamed she'd fall in love with the family. She thought of Brock's passionate kisses and soft murmurings. She'd lost her heart completely to each member of the family.

"What do I do now?" She kissed Tate's soft hair and lowered him to the changing table. Chicago and her old life were a vague memory compared to the realness she experienced being a part of this family. The only image that remained vivid in her mind was the night she lost her child. She'd played that day over and over in her head and still wasn't sure what she did to start labor and bring her child into the world before her small body was ready.

Her hands became numb and her face clammy as she relived the horror of trying to hold the contractions and the doctors rushing to try and save the premature baby. Where had Perry been? She couldn't remember. Her mother had driven her to the hospital. Did he ever show up other than to look at her with ridicule?

Her hands shook placing Tate on the bed and changing his diaper. She didn't believe any love was strong enough to sustain the devastation of a miscarriage. Perry blamed her. She saw it in his eyes. *Lord, she blamed herself.* She let the doctors, telling her everything was going great, lull her into doing things she probably shouldn't. She'd spent that morning helping her mother in the antique shop.

What was she thinking? She powdered Tate's chubby buttocks and taped the diaper up. Standing him in the crib, she pulled up his pants. Her heart twisted at the glee and trust sparkling in his eyes.

"I would have been a great mother!" she said, emphatically. Why couldn't this beautiful child be hers?

She slipped Tate's shirt over his head and tied his shoes. Picking him up, she headed downstairs. Just as she stepped into the kitchen, Brock and Willie T came through the back door.

"Willie T, what a pleasant surprise," she said, glad to have the older gentleman for a buffer between her and Brock.

"I was wondering if you would indulge an old man with a cup of coffee." He sniffed the air. "And pancakes."

"Wille T!" Maddie burst out of the kitchen at the sound of his voice. "You gonna take me on a field trip today?"

"He can't, Freckles, I need your help. Didn't Carina tell you?" Brock's gaze lingered on Carina longer than was proper with company and the children present.

"I'm sorry, I forgot to tell her. We had a discussion about dreams." Carina ducked into the kitchen, settling Tate in his high chair.

"Maddie, what did—" Brock admonished.

"She was full of decorum bringing up the topic." Carina jumped in to keep Maddie from getting in trouble.

Brock raised an eyebrow, but let it drop.

Carina let her breath out and handed Willie T a mug of coffee. "I hope you like it strong. Brock must have miscounted the scoops this morning," she said, smiling at the old man. He took the cup and flashed her a wide grin.

"I needed a strong cup this morning. I stayed up too late making a list of the things that need done around here." Brock took a sip and grimaced before continuing. "Maddie we're going to get that barn fixed up so you can ride in there this winter."

"Really? You've said that so many times." Her young face glowed with excitement.

"With Carina here to watch Tate, you'll have more spare time and improving your roping will benefit the ranch."

The joy on Maddie's face pushed Carina's objections aside. How could she ruin the child's happiness? But seeing Brock was in a generous mood, she decided to broach the riding question again.

"Would you feel better about giving me lessons if I rode inside?" She didn't know why, but learning to ride had become as desirable to her as staying with this family.

"We'll discuss it when the arena is finished." Brock shifted his attention to Willie T, and they discussed the clearing of the roads. Carina listened intently. Once the area was accessible Brock believed the social services would pay them a visit. She hoped it happened before she left, so Brock would get a good report.

"Come on Maddie, we've got work to do." Brock stood. "Willie T let Carina know which day of the week you'll be joining us for breakfast."

Carina studied the old man as Brock and Maddie left the kitchen. "You'll be joining us one day a week for breakfast?"

"It's a long story. Brock's a good man. He helps out those in need." His searching gaze made her wonder if he knew more about her than he let on.

"He is a good man. Too bad he doesn't have a wife to help him with his family." She gathered the dishes, carrying them to the sink. "Did you know his first wife, Beth?" She turned from the sink to see his expression.

"She was a delightful girl. Those two were sweet on each other from grade school." He glanced up. "We all knew they'd marry even though her father fought it."

"Why? Brock said her father didn't like him. I don't understand. Anyone can see he protects those he loves." Her heart squeezed. If only he'd been her husband when her life fell apart.

"Maxwell Johnson had a tough time of ranching.

He wanted more for his daughter. You could see from a young age Brock was bound to this land. He would spend hours herding cattle and camping." Willie T smiled. "That's when we met. He was wandering around out there in the middle of the night and came across me." The wrinkles around his eyes crinkled with mirth. "I was dressed in ceremonial clothes. Like to scared the black right out of his hair." The old man laughed, remembering the encounter.

His laughter was so infectious, that Carina joined in. Tate banged a spoon and laughed along with them.

Willie T wiped the tears from his eyes. "He's a good man. He deserves a good woman."

"Like Beth?" Carina asked, not knowing why she all of a sudden felt jealous of a woman she'd never known.

"No. Someone stronger, who can stand up to Brock and get these kids what they need beyond this ranch." The challenge in his eyes shocked her. He believed she was the one for Brock. But she had to go back to Chicago. To the life she knew.

Carina returned to the sink, turning the faucet handles, using the water to drown out the need to talk. Her mind raced. Did she truly deserve a man like Brock?

"Thank you for breakfast."

She heard a chair scrape the floor behind her.

Carina glanced over her shoulder. "You're welcome here anytime. Brock made that clear."

"What about you?" His dark eyes watched her intently.

"I enjoy your company as well." She smiled, moving from the sink and extending her hand. "You are a true friend of this family."

He captured her hand and smiled. "So are you."

A bolt of warmth surged through her. He pivoted, leaving the kitchen and the house while she stood in the same spot in the middle of the room. What had transpired between them? And why did she all of a sudden want to confess her problems?

Heaviness settled in her chest. If only she could unburden all the secrets she kept locked inside. She believed Brock would understand why she felt the need to keep the secret, but could he forgive her when she left?

Eleven

Carina stood at the kitchen sink when a small car came up the driveway. It was the first visitor besides Willie T they'd had in the two weeks she'd been at the ranch. Drying her hands, she picked Tate up off the floor where he'd been playing and headed to the front door.

She opened the door, letting in a gush of cold, fall air. Tate shuddered and by the warmth on her arm, wet his diaper. A gray-haired woman of ample girth and a dour expression huffed up to the porch steps.

"I'd like to speak with Brock Hughes." Her voice was raspy as a two-pack-a-day smoker.

"He's out checking the cattle." The censure in the woman's eyes said she had expected as much. "May I help you?"

"I'm Mrs. Corcoran of Social Services. I've received a complaint about Mr. Hughes leaving his children unattended for long periods of time." She eyed Carina. "Who are you?"

"I'm the children's nanny. And I can assure you,

Mr. Hughes does not leave his children unattended." Carina stepped back to allow the woman to enter. "Would you like a cup of coffee?" she asked, moving down the hall to the kitchen.

The woman appeared flustered at the offer of a beverage and was allowed into the house freely. She scanned every room she passed.

"I could use a cup of coffee after that drive." The woman settled her plumpness on one of the kitchen chairs and pulled a file from her satchel. "I don't have any record of Mr. Hughes employing a nanny."

Carina set the steaming mug in front of the woman and placed Tate in the high chair with a sippy cup. "Cookies?" she offered, picking up a plate of oatmeal cookies she'd made that morning.

Mrs. Corcoran's eyes lit up and she smacked her lips. "One would be good. It was a long drive." She took one, looked at the plate, and snatched another one. "A very long drive."

"Mr. Hughes hired me through the Exceptional Nannies organization. I can get you their card and any other information you need." Carina knew how to handle this type of person. They were so used to people trying to hoodwink and lie to them that being straightforward always threw them off.

"I'm sure we have their information at the office. How long have you been employed by Mr. Hughes?" Mrs. Corcoran licked her fingers and picked up a pen.

"I've been here nearly a month."

"And who was taking care of the children before that? I understand there hasn't been anyone other than the father around for nearly a year." She eyed the plate of cookies.

Carina pushed the plate closer to the woman. "A family friend helped look after the children until Mr. Hughes made up his mind about which nanny service to hire."

"I see." The woman took a cookie, dunked it in her coffee and scribbled on a paper. "And how long is your contract for?"

Carina couldn't look at the woman. She wasn't sure how long she'd be here. It could be only two more weeks. But she didn't dare tell the woman that. "It is open-ended, depending on Mr. Hughes satisfaction with my work and if the children and I get along."

Mrs. Cochran studied her shrewdly. "Are you having difficulties with the children?"

"Oh no! I was just stating the terms of the contract. The children are wonderful." Carina stroked Tate's cheek, and he smiled at her.

The woman smiled. "He seems smitten with you."

"Tate and I spend lots of time together. We've become very close."

The woman scanned a paper in front of her. "Where's Madeline?"

"She's out checking the cattle with her father." Carina smiled. The bond between the two grew daily. "They spend a good deal of time together. In the mornings, after Maddie's finished her school work, they work on getting the riding arena in shape, and in the afternoon, Mr. Hughes takes her along with him on his rounds of the pastures."

"So they're close?" Again, the woman eyed the cookies.

Carina smiled and pushed them even closer. "Yes. If something happened to come between them, it would devastate them both," she said while staring into the woman's eyes. She had to make it clear that taking Maddie from Brock was not in the best interest of the child or the father.

"I see." The woman put her pen down and clasped her hands together over her paperwork. "Do you know why I'm here?"

"Mr. Hughes mentioned something about Maddie's grandfather wants custody of her." Carina leaned forward, placing her hand on the woman's clasped hands. "Do you think taking a child from her father, someone she thinks the world of and loves with all her heart because an old man is lonely, is good for a child?"

The woman shook her head. "But I have to follow up on complaints. As far as I can see as long as you're here, Mr. Hughes has nothing to fear from Social Services."

Carina smiled at the woman. As long as she was here. How would Brock pay for her to stay on longer than the month?

Mrs. Corcoran put her papers back in her satchel, eyeing the cookies on the plate.

Carina retrieved a sandwich bag from the drawer and filled it with cookies. "It's a long drive back to Halverton," she said, handing the bag to the woman.

The smile the woman bestowed on her, told her Brock had nothing to fear from Social Services.

The next hour as she prepared dinner, Carina stewed over the prospect of Brock coming up with money for her wages. By the time the truck pulled into the drive she had a plan all formulated.

Maddie burst into the house. "I'm starving!" she wailed, kicking off her boots. She tossed her coat on a hook and washed her hands.

Tate toddled out to the mudroom flinging his arms around his sister's legs in a greeting.

"Hi Tate. What did you and Carina do while Daddy and I were gone?" She picked up her brother and wandered into the kitchen as Brock came through the door.

"Who was here?" he asked, hanging his coat and hat on a hook.

"How did you know someone was here?" Carina stared at the man. His hair, which needed cut, was flattened from wearing his hat all day, and his face was spattered with mud. And he was still the most handsome man she'd ever seen. Mentally slapping herself for such thoughts, she glanced down at his muddy boots on the off chance her emotions showed on her face.

"There are different tire tracks in the road, and they swung in from the county road side and not the ranch side."

"Where did you become so observant?"

His eyes darkened, and she realized she hit a nerve.

"It's one of the few things they didn't have to teach me in the military. Out here it's something you pick up."

"Well, the visitor was Mrs. Corcoran from Social Services." He looked at her with a hint of fear and a lot of rage on his face.

"They were supposed to call ahead and let me know someone was coming."

She put out a hand to soothe the anger she saw boiling up. "It's okay. She and I had a nice talk. I fed her cookies, and she went away feeling very favorable toward you and Maddie. She said as long as I remained taking care of the kids, she didn't see you having any problems with her organization."

He stared at her as if he didn't believe what she'd just told him. "She went away saying that?"

"Yes. I made a very good impression. Either that or it was the cookies." Carina smiled, trying to get Brock to do the same.

"We aren't going to be hounded by them anymore?" He scooped her into an embrace and swung her around.

"Brock." Before she could say any more his lips captured hers. She forgot about the woman, the kids, and anything else. The magic his lips possessed sent shock waves of delight dancing from her lips to her toes.

The clanging of dishes brought her sense back. Pushing against his chest, she reluctantly pulled out of his embrace.

"Dinner's ready," she said not daring to look at him and headed into the kitchen. That kiss felt wonderful—yet, was inappropriate. She was the nanny and would be nothing more. Couldn't be anything more.

Brock wandered into the kitchen perplexed and happy. Carina had charmed the social worker. Her pulling out of his embrace puzzled him. She'd just started to melt in his arms, then stiffened and pulled away. It had been the excitement over the news that pushed him to be so bold. Surely, she didn't take it as anything else? Did she? He'd never take things to that level. He couldn't. She was only here as long as he could pay for her.

"I had a thought, well actually, you brought it up on the trip to Dutch Springs." Brock studied Carina as she raised a lid on a pot of steaming potatoes. "How do I go about selling some of these antiques so I can keep you here longer?"

Maddie flung her arms around his waist. "Daddy, really? We can keep Carina?"

Brock smiled at his ecstatic child and patted her head. "We have a few things around here that only collect dust and don't mean that much to me. If we sell them, we can keep Carina around a little longer." He watched the woman standing by the sink, biting her bottom lip.

"What do you say? Will you help me sell some things?" His heart pounded with trepidation. The expression on her face didn't reveal the excitement he'd expected. She had to stay. The social worker required it for him to keep his daughter.

"I'll help you sell some furniture and I'll stay, but we have to set some ground rules." From the look in her eyes and the steel in her voice, he knew one of them was going to be no kissing. The prospect wilted his male ego, but he knew it was for the best. He shouldn't have come on so strong, but lately the pain of the past had blurred.

"We'll work on the rules later. What do I need to do first?" He grabbed a pad of paper from the drawer of miscellaneous items and sat down at the table.

"Make a list of the items you don't mind parting with." She hesitated and winced slightly. "I'll call my mother, and see what she says. She'll know who to contact about the different pieces. Once a sale has been made, we ship it directly to the buyer, with them paying the shipping."

"It can go that smoothly?" He stopped writing. "How much do you think we can get?"

"It depends on the items. My mother would be a better judge of that."

"Here's what I have so far." He pushed the list across the table. She approached the table and paper as though it were a bomb. "It won't bite." How could one innocent kiss have her acting like her staying on was a death sentence?

"It—" She looked over her shoulder at Maddie. "Sweetie, why don't you take Tate upstairs for his nap?"

Brock saw the light go on in his daughter's head. She realized Carina had something she didn't want to say in front of her.

"Sure." Maddie scooped up her brother and marched out the door, winking at him as she passed.

Brock snickered. Carina faced him. The agony he'd witnessed moments before in her eyes, snapped to anger.

"You find this funny? That you have to sell your family heirlooms to keep a nanny."

"No. I'm laughing at my daughter." He rubbed the back of his neck. *Damn.* This wasn't the time to get another headache. He needed a clear head.

She moved behind him. He turned to see what she was about when her small hands massaged his tense neck muscles. The heat of her fingers kneading and smoothing the muscle relaxed his whole body. He closed his eyes and dreamed of a time when he had little on his mind. Before the damn war and Beth's death.

Her scent drifted to his slow breathing. Beth's scent, Beth's hands. He grasped the small hand in his and pulled it down to kiss the magic fingers. Her hand trembled when he kissed each finger. His loins flamed with need. Turning her hand palm up, he kissed the small, soft pad. Where was the rough calluses he remembered?

Brock opened his eyes and stared down at the small hand he held. It wasn't Beth's. He dropped her hand and stood, scooting the table forward.

"I'm sorry. I—" He spun and stared into the eyes of a woman other than the one he'd dreamed of. The confusion in their blue depths turned to embarrassment.

"No, I…I was just trying to help." She turned to leave.

"Use the phone in my office to call your mom." He picked up the list of furniture, holding it out to her.

Carina didn't know what to do. She'd seen the pain on his face as he rubbed his neck and knew she could help. When her hands touched his body, she lost all sense of time and place. All she wanted was to continue to touch and soothe him. When he kissed her fingers— God help her, her insides clenched. *She wanted him*.

"I don't think staying here longer than a month is a good idea." She stepped away from the extended paper and the fury she expected to erupt.

"You're right. We need to set ground rules."

"No. I need to leave when the month is up." Here it came. She saw the rage building.

"No! I'll not touch you again." He paced to the sink, crumpling the paper in his clenching fist. "You can't leave. You yourself said the social services will leave us alone as long as you're here. And I get more done with you watching Tate and Maddie." He stalked back and shoved the paper in her face. "You call and find out how to get the money to pay the agency. I promise I won't lay a hand on you if you stay."

The rental car sat by the barn covered in dust. She could leave any time. Carina watched the man looming over her. He didn't scare her. She knew he wouldn't physically hurt her, and he wouldn't forcefully make her stay. *So walk out the door.*

She took the paper and pivoted on her heels. The children needed her. She wouldn't let some vengeful man take these children from a loving father. That was the only reason she didn't put the key in the ignition of the dusty sports car.

Yeah, keep telling yourself that.

Twelve

After dinner, Carina took a deep breath and dialed her mother's number. Their last conversation had been filled with weeping and pleading on her mother's part. The phone trilled in her ear. Maybe she wasn't home? She could leave a short message and get a better grip on her emotions before she talked to the woman.

"Hello?" said her out of breath mother.

"Mom. It's me." Tears burned in her eyes at the happy shriek from her parent.

"Carina. Oh darling, I've been so worried. I didn't care what Georgie said, I still needed to hear you're well from you."

"I'm doing fine." *As good as could be expected having fallen in love with your employer and his children.*

"I'm so glad! Tell me all about the family you're working for. And don't leave out any of the details." She heard her mother moving. Ever since she bought her the cordless phone, her mom would make tea while she talked and then sit in her favorite antique chair and sip while she listened. These were the same actions of her childhood. Carina would come home full of the exploits from her day; her mother went through the same routine of tea and her favorite chair. The memories warmed and made her melancholy for the innocent days of her youth.

Carina told her of the children. How smart and fun they were and giving a brief sketch of Brock.

"Oh, they all sound delightful! Will you be able to come home for the holidays?"

The idea hadn't crossed her mind. Holidays weren't something she relished since losing her child. Her thoughts lingered on her mother's excitement when she thought she'd have a grandchild to shop for. The ache which had started to ebb now emerged to strangle her heart.

"I don't know, Mom."

"Surely, your employer can tend the children while you come home to us. You have to be here. Otherwise—I'll have no one." She heard the tears in her mother's voice.

"I'll see. Mom, what I really called about is selling some antiques."

"You don't have any antiques. Your apartment looks like a junk dealer's retreat."

"You know that apartment was temporary, and I didn't have the funds to furnish it. The antiques belong to my employer. He would like to sell some." She didn't want to tell her mother why. Helping the man sell his heirlooms, she secured a place by his side for a while longer. Something she both cherished and feared.

"I can't help if I can't see them. E-mail me some pictures along with information about the pieces, and

I'll shop them around." She swallowed. "Is the only reason you called because of this?"

Carina slumped in the chair. Lie and make her mother feel better or tell the truth?

"No, mom. There was a storm the day I arrived and they just fixed the phone lines."

"You have a cell phone which I have tried numerous times."

"This is a remote area. My cell phone doesn't work out here."

"Then how did you call Georgie?" The accusation in her mother's voice made her feel eleven again.

"Mom, I was on the phone with Georgie to tell her I made it when the phone went out." She rubbed her temple, wanting the conversation to end.

"Give me your number there so I can contact you after you send the photos."

This was her mom's way of being able to contact her whenever she wanted. She loved her mother, but she was part of the reason for the drastic change in her lifestyle. Her clinginess.

"Okay." She recited the number and hoped Brock didn't mind her mother calling several times a day from here on out.

"It was so good to hear your voice, darling."

"You, too, Mom."

"I love you and miss my only living relative."

"I know. I love you, too. Take care and I'll send those pictures as soon as I can." Carina hung up the phone wishing she'd had siblings for her mother to expend some love upon.

She stretched and listened. The house was dark and quiet. Brock headed up the stairs to put the children to bed when she entered the office to make the phone call. She didn't want to venture out of the safety of the office and run into the man. Dinner had been a silent, awkward meal. Even Maddie hadn't chattered.

If she planned to stay on after her month, there had to be rules put in place. She opened the desk drawer, pulling out a sheet of paper and pen. Tapping the pen against her chin, she tried to think of what would constitute a good rule.

The only one she could think of was the one which brought her body back to life. She couldn't write that down on paper. What if Maddie came across the paper?

She stood, squared her shoulders, and knew what had to be done. Her mouth went dry as she climbed the stairs to the second floor and knocked on Brock's door.

He didn't open the door with abandon as he had the first night of her arrival. The door opened enough for him to stick his head out.

She cleared her throat. "We need to talk."

He glared at her. "What about?"

"The rules we need if I'm going to stay." She didn't dare allow her gaze to drift anywhere other than his eyes.

The door opened and he waved her to enter. She scanned down his bare chest to the top of his low-riding, flannel pj bottoms. The man had the most perfect abs she'd ever seen. Swallowing the spit building in her mouth, she jerked her gaze back up to his face. The smirk on his face stimulated the anger she needed.

"Put a shirt on and follow me down to the living room," she said, pivoting to leave.

"Why can't we discuss this here?"

"I don't want Maddie to hear the conversation."

"Do you plan to yell?" The snicker in his voice had her hands clenching.

"No. However, you should know her well enough to know she wanders around at night awake checking on you and Tate. I don't want her checking on you and finding me in your room."

His chin dropped nearly to his chest. She smiled smugly and headed for the stairs. He'd meet her in the living room and have questions. He didn't even know his daughter looked in on him. Just like a man. Perry slept through everything, too. How many nights had she tried waking him after having nightmares… Shivers wracked her body. This wasn't the time to think about the pain and guilt.

She turned on a light, sat on the straight-backed chair next to the sofa, and waited.

Brock stepped off the last stair softly so as not to arouse Carina, who appeared deep in thought. The single lamp illuminated the lines around her eyes and at the corners of her mouth. Whatever she was thinking brought her pain. Panic hit him. *She planned to leave.* He needed her to keep this family together. If she wasn't here Johnson would win.

She couldn't leave. He'd agree to all her rules. And whatever it took to keep his family together and Carina in his house. The last thought hit him like a slap across the face. He didn't want her here solely for the family. His days wouldn't be filled with her smiles and optimism if she left.

Taking a stance to the side of her chair, he cleared his throat. Her head snapped around and a swear word whispered out between her parted lips.

Brock chuckled. So his prim and proper nanny could utter a cuss word.

"Don't sneak up on me like that." She pulled her legs up under her on the chair in a protective gesture.

"I wasn't sneaking. You told me to come down and I did. I can't help it if you were off somewhere else."

The snap in her eyes lessened as she pushed her unbound hair away from her face. "I'm sorry. I'm so confused right now." Her shoulders sagged.

Brock lowered to sit on the edge of the sofa. He leaned forward, tipping her chin with a finger so he could see what emotions swirled on her face.

She pulled back. "That's the first rule." Her back straightened. "Don't touch me."

Brock yanked his hand back. "I don't understand? I won't hurt you." Did she despise him so much?

She sighed, but wouldn't meet his gaze. "I know. Just, please, don't touch me." Her chest heaved under the tight, blue sweater he'd admired all day. "I'll stay as the children's nanny if you don't touch me in any fashion while I'm here."

He started to make a comment, but she raised her hand to stop him.

"I can't give you any clarifying answer other than, it is a rule I want established." She glanced at him and quickly looked away, her cheeks flushed and lashes lowered.

He smiled. This had to do with their kisses. She didn't want to get involved knowing she would leave when her services were no longer needed.

He understood her reasoning. It made sense, not only for her, but himself as well. Letting her into his home was enough, he didn't have room to let her into his heart. Beth and the kids were all he had room for. Though, he wouldn't mind relieving the ache in his loins with Carina.

At the thought, he hardened and his face flushed. He cleared his throat and rose to stand by the fireplace. With his back to her he said, "I'll follow your rule. Are there any others?"

"Not that I can think of at the moment."

"Then I'm going to bed." He turned from the fireplace and strode across the room, stopping at the bottom of the stairway. "Good night." Without waiting for a response, he took the stairs two at a time. He headed straight to the shower to douse his body in cold water just as he had as a teenager when he lusted after Beth.

Thirteen

Brock pulled off his cowboy hat and wiped at the sweat beading on his forehead. For the last week every morning after checking on the cattle, he and Maddie worked on the indoor arena. It hadn't been used since Beth's accident. Boards hung loose around the edge and leaks in the roof had packed the ground in a couple of spots.

He stood back looking at the area. Why had he let this go? Her accident hadn't happened here. *You let more than this arena deteriorate since her death.* His conscience was right. He'd also let his heart shrink. Until Carina showed up. He smiled thinking of her cooking and taking care of Tate. Watching her every day and not touching was the hardest thing he'd ever done, but he'd followed her rule and wasn't going to make things harder if she decided to leave.

Just thinking of her leaving was like a punch to his gut.

"Daddy! Can I ride in here now?" Maddie entered the arena leading her mare, Cookie.

"It's all yours," he said, picking up the last of the tools. He stepped out of the building and into a flurry of snowflakes. *Damn.* The weather forecasters had been right for a change. He'd hoped the snow would hold off a couple more weeks. Good thing he had the arena finished. The cows would require feeding and closer watch since they were due to start calving.

Carina stepped out of the house bundled in a coat and gazing up at the large flakes floating out of the sky.

Brock smiled and detoured toward her. "You get snow in Chicago," he said, watching with fascination the joy on her face.

"Sure. But it isn't the same. These are pure snowflakes falling on wide open spaces." She pointed to a flake on the ground. "You wouldn't get a chance to see that single flake in the city. It would be trod on or run over by a car or bicycle before you could notice its perfection."

Perfection. That was the woman admiring the snowflake. "How does someone so wrapped up in the small things in life survive in the city?"

She glanced at him and smiled, warming him and hugging his heart. "You look for those little things that make you happy and cling to them." She nodded to the arena. "Is it done?"

"Yeah, Maddie's taking a spin on Cookie."

"Can I see?" she asked, apprehension shining in her eyes.

Did she think he wouldn't allow her in the building? "Sure. Let me put these tools away." He walked over to the shed, putting the tools in their proper place, and joined her at the entrance to the arena. The muffled thud of hooves in the worked-up ground, the creak of leather, and the snorting horse echoed in the large building as the girl and horse cantered around the pen.

Carina walked to the gate and peered over. Maddie and her horse went round and around the soft, dirt floor. They moved effortlessly. Watching the two made her yearn to ride even more.

She glanced at Brock standing beside her. A loving smile tipped the corners of his lips as his gaze followed Maddie. Did he see his beloved Beth? Would asking to ride make him think she was trying to be like his deceased wife? She didn't care what he thought. She wanted to ride a horse and be as free and happy as Maddie looked at this moment.

She cleared her throat and asked, "Now that the arena is finished, could you teach me to ride?"

His smile faded.

He continued to watch Maddie. "Now that the snow is here, I'll have to feed the cows and check on them more often. The first calves are due soon."

She grabbed his arm and pulled him around to look at her. "Why do you refuse to teach me to ride? If I'm here in the arena and you are present, how can anything happen to me?"

"Why do you want to ride?" His voice was gruff.

"I've always wondered what it would be like." She watched Maddie glide by. "It looks like fun and something I think I would be good at."

Willie T entered the building. "You must have finished. I hear the sound of hooves." He stopped beside them. Carina forced a smile.

Brock faced the old man. "You have great timing."

"No, he doesn't," Carina said, shoving her hands

on her hips and squaring up in front of Brock.

"Ah, what is this squabble about?" Willie T asked, smiling.

The smile and the sparkle in the old man's eyes only fueled her anger. "This man is being stupid and obstinate."

"I'm being practical."

"No, you aren't. I have given you twenty-four/seven nanny service. The least you can do is give me riding lessons."

"So, that is what this is about." Willie T whistled and Maddie and Cookie came over to the gate. "Come on. Let's go see what your brother is doing. Your father and Carina need time to work something out."

"I'll go with you," Carina said, moving out of the way of the gate as Maddie dismounted and walked through.

"No." Willie T put up his hand. "You will stay here and get this talked out. From what I can see, it's something you both feel strongly about. You both need to see the other's side and clear the air."

Brock glared at the man, while Carina watched both men. Was this something they planned? She wouldn't doubt it. Willie T probably didn't think she should ride either. Thinking both men ganged up on her only angered her more. The nerve of the two thinking they knew what was best for her. They didn't even know her.

When Willie T and Maddie left the building, she faced Brock. His mouth was set in a firm line as he stared out at the arena. His jaw twitched.

She grabbed the sleeve of his coat and pulled him around to look at her. "Did you put him up to this?"

"Up to what?" he growled, glowering down at her.

"Don't tell me he isn't on your side about me learning to ride." Shoving her hands on her hips again, she tilted back on her heels to glare up into his challenging eyes.

"Willie T doesn't take sides." Brock's heated gaze scanned her body. "You don't need to learn how to ride. It won't do you any good when you go back to Chicago."

"You don't care what I do when I leave here. You just don't want to teach me. Fine. I'll ask Willie T, and you'll be free to tend your cows."

He glared at her. The twitch in his jaw became more pronounced. "Willie T won't teach you either."

"Why not?" Why was he being so…so *infuriating*?

"Because I'll ask him not to."

"Why? What is wrong with me learning to ride?"

He stood still, staring at her, his eyes unflinching.

She sighed. "Why can't you see this is just something I want to do? I'm not trying to be like Beth or take her place."

"You couldn't."

His words sent shards of ice piercing her heart. *That was it*. He thought she tried to be Beth in every way. Tears formed before she could turn away.

"Damn. I didn't mean it that way." He wrapped his arms around her, drawing her against him. Kissing the top of her head, he moaned. "You are fire where Beth was a soft breeze. I have never compared you to Beth. I only see you for the passionate, full-of-life woman you are."

Carina's heart thudded in her chest. "Then why won't you let me ride?"

"I don't want to lose you too." The agony in his words sliced through her anger. Her resolve to remain unaffected by him slipped out of her grasp.

"You can't possibly lose me by my riding a horse around an arena. I'll just keep going around and around in a circle with no way out." Her attempt at humor lifted the corners of Brock's mouth.

"You are one sassy woman," he said, kissing her neck.

"And you're one stubborn man." Carina wound her hands in the hair at the back of his neck, knocking his hat to the ground, and dragging his lips to hers.

The fire that fused their lips buckled her knees. Sagging against him, she locked her arms around his neck. He scooped her into his arms. She continued kissing him while he carried her to the stall where the hay was stacked.

He lowered her to the bales, lying down next to her. "I've wanted to kiss you like this for a long time," he said, running his hands through her hair and drawing her mouth to his.

The softness of his lips and urgency of his kiss made her lightheaded and yearning for more. His mouth traveled from her lips to her jaw, down her neck. Oh, the glorious sensations his touch spiraled through her.

She ripped the snaps open on his coat, needing to touch his skin. Dragging his shirt tails out of his pants, she slid her hands under the shirt and across the firm muscles of his back.

"I've dreamed of this," he whispered, pushing her coat aside and lifting her T-shirt. Her breath caught when the cold air touched her skin followed by his warm, strong hands sliding up her sides. Her nipples tightened and tingled when he slid his hands behind her, releasing her bra.

Brock was amazed at how her breasts filled his hands. The erect nipples begged to be kissed. He leaned down, taking one in his mouth. Carina wiggled under him, her moan of appreciation driving him to give the other breast his attention.

She grabbed his shirt, ripping the snaps open. He pulled back. The look of rapture in her eyes as her hands explored his chest took him over the brink of rationalization. He didn't care if they were in the barn in the hay. *He had to have her.*

Her slender hands trailed down his torso to the top of his Wranglers.

Now.

He pulled her shirt and bra over her head. Her full breasts and soft curves took his breath away. He leaned down, giving her full, sweet lips the attention they deserved.

"Daddy!"

His head jerked up, and he froze gazing down at Carina, stripped to her waist.

"Daddy!" The shout rang clearer.

"Damn!" Brock's heart pounded in his chest as fear stronger than anything he'd ever felt gripped him. He didn't want his young daughter to find him ravaging a naked woman in the barn. He jumped off the bale, snapping his shirt and tucking it in.

Carina scrambled to get dressed as well.

"I'm sorry," he said, snapping his coat and hurrying away. That was why they had the rule no touching. *Damn!*

He stepped out of the barn and relief spread

through him. Maddie still stood on the porch. Carina would have time to get herself together.

"What?" He hurried to the house through the curtain of snowflakes falling.

"Grandpa's on the phone."

His heart stopped and anger surged through his veins. What did the sour man want? He glanced back at the barn, Carina just emerged. Hay clung to her hair. He hoped she could come up with a good story; he had other matters to take care of.

Entering the house, he didn't even glance at Willie T. The thought of talking with his father-in-law didn't sit well with him. He picked up the receiver from the counter where Maddie had placed it.

"Yes," he said, in a less than genial voice.

"I began to think you weren't even going to take the call."

"I was in the barn. What do you want?" He could barely keep the resentment out of his voice. Mr. Johnson had not changed a bit. His words were razor-sharp and nicked Brock's pride just like always.

"With the snow, this could be a hard winter. I've got someone interested in your ranch. He's got lots of money and would pay you more than that place is worth." The contemptuous tone of his voice set Brock's hair on end.

"You know good-n-well this place isn't for sale. And it never will be as long as I'm alive."

"That's something to consider after the way you took care of my daughter."

"What's that supposed to mean?" Fury washed through him, causing his head to whoosh and his hand to clench the phone.

"You know what I'm talking about. And how about the way you're raising my grandchild."

"Since when have you cared a twit about Maddie?"

"Since I heard you've got some slut living there."

That did it. This man had never met Carina and hadn't given a crap about his granddaughter for five years.

"*Mr*. Johnson, I will never sell, and I will bring *my* daughter up as I see fit. How I do that is my concern and not yours." Brock slammed the phone down.

His vision blurred. He stared around the room not seeing anyone or anything. The fury in him raged. The man had some balls to call here trying to sell his family's home and tell him how to raise his daughter.

Carina entered at the end of the conversation. She glanced at Maddie. The child's sad and fearful gaze on her father tightened Carina's chest. Moving across the room, she stood beside the girl, hugging her.

Willie T sat stone still watching Brock. Carina cleared her throat. Brock shook like a dog coming out of water. His eyes cleared, and he stared at Maddie.

"I'm so sorry you heard all of that, Freckles." He moved across the room, hugging his daughter tight. "Your grandfather is trying to get me to sell again."

"We'll never sell," Maddie said with vigor.

"No, we never will."

Carina's eyes watered watching the two clinging to one another. Selling the ranch would pull them apart.

Tate's cries floated down the stairs. "I'll get him," Carina said.

"No. Maddie, will you get Tate? I want to talk to Willie T and Carina." Brock nodded his head toward the kitchen door.

Maddie nodded and left the room.

Carina saw the anger returning to Brock's eyes. He paced the kitchen, running a hand through his hair.

"That son-of-a-bitch Johnson said he had a buyer for the ranch. Insinuating I'm not going to make it through the winter." He slammed a fist into his palm. His gaze rested on Carina and his face reddened.

"I've been keeping this from you, and I'm sorry now. If you want to leave," he cleared his throat, "especially after this afternoon, I'll understand."

Carina glanced at Willie T and back to Brock. What was he talking about? That they broke the one rule she was so adamant they keep? It had been as much her fault as his. Once his arms came around her, she couldn't think of anything other than finding solace in his embrace.

"The people of Dutch Springs say I'm paying you in," he looked at Willie T and ran a hand over his face "in bed privileges."

"That's…that's…" She saw where this afternoon would play into the rumors. Her heart sunk in her chest. "My…" She lowered herself onto a chair. "Why? Why would they think that?"

"They all know I'm in debt from Beth's medical bills. And can't see how I could afford a nanny." He watched her. Concern in the brown depths of his eyes, warmed her, taking away her shame.

He faced the old man sitting at the table watching them. "Willie T will you and Jack take some of my antiques to Halverton tomorrow and sell them?"

"No, you won't get near what they're worth if you do that," Carina chimed in.

"I need to have people see I'm selling, so they

know I'm paying you." He captured her arm. "I won't have them spread rumors about you."

"What about you? It would be bad for Maddie to hear…you know about her father."

"I'm not worried about Maddie. She lives here and knows what she sees."

Carina blushed. She'd almost seen too much this afternoon. Brock also colored a little.

"I tried to tell her to take a message," Willie T cut in, his eyes shining with mirth.

They both turned and stared at the old man, who just lifted a mug of coffee to his smiling lips.

Carina shook her head and smiled. The old man was craftier than he looked.

"How fast can I get money from the furniture?" Brock asked, breaking into her thoughts.

"We should have taken photos when I first called my mother." She studied Brock. "You'll get more money and won't have to sell as many."

"All I have is an old camera." Brock rubbed the back of his neck.

"I'll drive into Halverton tomorrow and buy a digital camera. That way we can send the photos and have offers within a couple of days."

"Have you driven in snow before?" Brock took a step toward her concern creased his forehead.

"No, but I'll go slow." She bit her lip. There was no way she'd pull Brock from his chores to take her to town.

"If you haven't driven in snow this isn't the time to learn."

Carina looked at Willie T. "Tell him I can drive to town?"

"I would offer to take you, but I have to take my daughter to the doctor in Boise tomorrow." Willie T shrugged and looked apologetic.

Carina faced Brock. "You need to take care of the cows. I'll be fine. I'll leave mid-morning and be back by dark." She scanned Brock's face, lingering on his mouth. Heat simmered in her core at the thought of the kisses they'd shared in the barn.

"You don't know how to drive in snow. What happens if you end up in a ditch? Locating and pulling you out will cost me more time than driving you there."

She figured he'd be stubborn about this.

"The children can stay here so you don't have to worry about them. I'm an adult and will go to Halverton of my own accord." She put her hands on her hips and challenged him to argue the point.

"Fine, go to Halverton, but you will follow Willie T since he has to go through Halverton to get to Boise. And if he says you can't head back on your own…you stay there until someone comes and gets you." Brock stared at her, waiting for an answer.

The thought of following Willie T was a relief. For all her bravado, she really wasn't excited to have her first outing in snow all alone.

"I'll go for that."

He pointed with his thumb to his chest, "And I'm buying the camera."

"I'll purchase the camera. I don't have a mortgage that needs paid and children to feed."

His jaw twitched. It hurt his male pride to know she was right.

"Besides, I've wanted to take pictures."

Brock glanced from her to Willie T. "But I'll pay

you back when I get money from the antiques."

Carina put her hand out. He wrapped his long fingers around hers. "Deal."

"Can Tate and I come down now?" Maddie called from the top of the stairs.

"Yes!" Brock called back.

Carina smiled at Willie T. "What time do we leave in the morning?"

Fourteen

Willie T and his daughter drove in front of the house and honked the horn as Carina finished giving Maddie instructions.

"Carina, we've been home alone before, and Daddy said he'd come by several times to check on us. Go. Don't worry about us, just watch the road," Maddie said with a smile. The concern on the child's face did little to stop the nausea that had lingered since Carina woke.

"I'll take my time. Don't worry if I'm not back when you think I should be, I'll drive slow." Carina kissed them on the head, grabbed her coat and purse, and dashed out through the falling snow to Brock's truck. He'd insisted she use the truck rather than the rented sports car, showing her how to put it in four-wheel drive if she needed.

He'd started the vehicle before jumping in with Jack to check the cows. The truck was warm inside, though it smelled a bit like dog and cattle.

She waved at Willie T to go and followed him out

the drive and onto the county road. The sparse traffic on the gravel road made traveling easy. So far so good.

At the stop sign to pull onto the highway, the wheels spun and the back end of the vehicle swerved. Carina clenched the steering wheel, turning her knuckles white and tried to keep up with Willie T. After the shaky start on the snow-packed road, she wasn't eager to go as fast as the skilled man ahead of her.

Knots bunched in her back and a pin-pricking headache irritated her senses by the time they hit the outskirts of town two hours later. Carina shook out her shoulders when the tires met pavement. She loosened the death grip on the steering wheel and took a deep breath. Willie T pulled into the parking lot of a chain store she recognized. She pulled to a stop alongside his vehicle and rolled the window down.

"You did fine. Just be sure to go that slow on the way back." He put a hand through the open window and patted her clenched fingers. "Relax. The key to good driving in snow is remaining relaxed."

She slowly unwrapped her hand from the steering wheel. Her fingers ached when she tried to straighten them.

"I'll try to remember that." She rolled her head to relieve the tension and flashed a weak smile at Willie T.

He returned the smile and headed to his vehicle. Opening the door, he turned. "See you the day after tomorrow."

She should have known he wouldn't forget to show up for his weekly breakfast.

Laughing, she pulled on her coat and picked up her purse. *Time to buy a camera.* She knew Brock didn't like her purchasing the instrument to help pay for her services, however, she wanted photos of the area—and family—to look back on in years to come. And she was willing to dip into her savings to help Brock keep his family together.

"There isn't much variety," she said to the woman behind the counter who had less experience with the devices than Carina. "And I'm not familiar with most of these brands."

She contemplated calling Georgie. Her friend worked in a field that dealt with digital photos. Did she dare risk running down the battery in her phone? Of course, if she considered the fact that her phone would be useless for over half the trip back to the ranch…

Popping the case open, her finger hovered over the speed dial button. Before the miscarriage and divorce she didn't need anyone else's opinion to make a decision. But since then, it seemed she couldn't think on her own. That had to stop. Carina clicked the phone shut and pointed to the most expensive camera. "I'll take that one."

Before the loss of her baby, she was always in control—whether a challenging student or a chaotic staff meeting. The trek over the snow-packed road and purchasing the camera were the first challenges she'd tackled since that devastating day.

Smiling, she turned from the counter with her purchase dangling in the bag in her hand.

The distressed cry of a newborn shook her bravado. Frantically, she looked around for the child. A harried-looking teenager pushed a cart past, shushing the baby and nearly smothering it with a blanket.

Save the baby. "No!" Carina dashed after the young mother. She ripped the blanket off the baby and fumbled with trying to unhook the straps holding it in the carrier.

"Leave my baby alone!" screamed the mother, pulling on Carina's arms.

"You can't harm this baby. You can't!" Carina choked as tears streamed down her face. She had to save it.

"Lady! Leave the baby alone." The male voice and tight grasp around her arm shook Carina. The hand propelled her away from the excited mother and crying child.

Oh my God! What have I done! I would have taken that woman's baby and—what?

Carina swiped the tears from her face and jerked out of the man's grasp. He'd pulled her out onto the sidewalk in front of the store. The glare of the sun on the snow made her squint as she tried to get a look at the man who intervened. In the distance, a siren pierced the cold air and steadily grew in volume.

She shivered. After all this time and distance, she thought the past had been put to rest. But she couldn't let it rest.

A police car slid into the parking lot. The man next to her waved his hand and grabbed her arm, again.

"Let go of me!" She tried to yank free.

"I ain't letting no baby snatcher get away," he said, gripping her arm tighter.

"I'm not a *baby snatcher*." She glared at the man. He was older and not quite as tall as Brock. His grip was like steel on her arm. "I won't run away. I didn't mean to frighten the girl." She tried to relax so the man would see she wouldn't bolt.

The officer approached them with his thumbs

resting on the front of his belt. "Heard we had a baby snatching." He didn't look old enough to be out of school.

"Please, listen. It wasn't baby snatching. I just over-reacted when I saw how the young woman handled the baby." She looked from one man to the other. "I'm a nanny and when I see children in distress, I react." She had to get back to the ranch without Brock learning about this.

"I haven't heard of anyone around here having a nanny." The youthful officer narrowed his eyes and put a hand on his handcuffs.

Brock didn't need to get involved. "I'm not working for anyone in town."

The man still holding her arm snapped his fingers. "I heard Brock Hughes has a nanny." He looked her up and down and whistled. "Dang, wish I had a nanny like you."

"Well, you don't." She pulled her arm from his grip and turned to the officer. "Look, it was a misunderstanding on my part. I thought the child was in danger and reacted. I'm sorry if I caused the mother any trauma. I was merely reacting on instinct."

"Do you work for Brock Hughes?" The officer pulled a small notepad out of his coat pocket.

"Yes. And he's expecting me to return home by a certain time or come looking for me. I really don't want to pull him away from his duties at the ranch." She put a hand on the door of the truck.

"That's Brock's pickup. I worked on it last summer when Maddie drove it into the creek and gunked it all up," her abductor said, smiling and nodding his head.

"And that's exactly why I'm there. To make sure

Maddie doesn't drive vehicles and Tate is taken care of so Maddie can do her school work." Carina opened the door, tossing the bag with the camera and her purse on the seat.

The officer moved quickly to the vehicle. "Where do you think you're going?"

"To pick up some items at the grocery store and then head back to the ranch." Carina put the key in the ignition.

"Not until I have a full report. You'll have to come to the station with me." He opened the door and took her by the arm.

"But I said it was all a misunderstanding."

"That's what *you* say. I have witnesses that say otherwise."

Carina rolled her eyes, grabbed her purse, and slid out of the truck.

"Jason, drive this pickup over to the station. No sense in impounding until we know if we're keeping her or not." The officer tossed the keys to the man who dragged her out of the store.

"I have to get back before dark otherwise Maddie will be worried." Carina turned to the officer. "Please, just let me get my groceries and go back to the ranch. I promise not to set foot in Halverton again if that will make you happy. I wasn't trying to snatch the baby. I wanted to help it." The pleading in her voice shocked her. She'd never stooped this low, using her feminine wiles to get out of a sticky situation, but right now she would do anything to keep Brock and his family from finding out about her lapse in judgment.

"I didn't say we'd book you. I just would like more information." He opened the police car door and motioned for her to get in.

Carina sighed and fell onto the seat. If she cooperated, she still might make it back home without the family finding out.

***

The grandfather clock bonged through the house as Brock entered the back door. He'd grab a quick sandwich, load up the kids in Jack's pickup, and head back out to feed the older cows. The heifers were all resting comfortably. Another week and they would start birthing.

"Maddie! Get Tate dressed. I'm taking you two with me!" Brock washed his hands and dealt slices of bread onto the counter. He pulled the cupboard door open and the phone rang.

"I'll get it!" he called, crossing the room and snatching up the phone. "Yeah."

"Brock?"

His good mood turned sour. "Yeah, it's me, Johnson. Why do you sound so surprised? Did you sell my place without my knowing it?"

"I didn't expect to find you there. Your pickup is parked in front of the police station." The question in his voice wasn't going to get answered.

"I loaned my pickup out." Anger was replaced with worry. Why would Carina go to the police station?

"To that mutt you call a hired hand?"

"Who I hire is none of your business and neither is who has my pickup." Brock hung up the phone as Maddie entered carrying her brother.

"Grandpa, again?"

"How do you know that?" Brock went back to spreading peanut butter.

"Cuz your face is always red after talking to him and you look about ready to knock a hole in the wall." She grinned, and he couldn't help but smile back.

"You are too darn observant." He pointed to the high chair. "Dump Tate in there and help me get these sandwiches made."

When Maddie spooned jam onto the bread, Brock casually asked, "Did Carina say if she was going to do anything other than buy a camera?"

"She mentioned picking up some stuff at the grocery store." She stopped in the middle of licking her finger. "Don't worry Daddy. She's only getting a couple of things. She knows not to spend a lot of money."

"I'm not worried she'll spend money." Brock topped the sandwiches and shoved them in baggies.

"Take Tate out to the pickup and I'll bring lunch." When the door closed behind Maddie and her charge, he dialed the Halverton police station.

"This is Brock Hughes. Can you tell me why my pickup is in front of the station?" He listened as the woman went into detail of how they caught a baby snatcher.

When the woman stopped for a breath he asked, "What's this baby snatcher look like?"

"She's tiny. You'd think someone that size wouldn't be strong enough to run with a child. Dark brown hair with a little red in it. You know, they say redheads are unstable. Just look at that wacko Carrot Top fellow on the commercials."

"Can I talk to the officer who brought her in?" The knot started forming at the back of his neck. What happened? Carina would never harm a child.

"This is Officer Warren."

The young voice squelched his fears. "I understand you have my nanny in custody."

"This Brock Hughes?" The shock in the man's voice told Brock they didn't believe anything Carina said.

"Yes. I'm Brock Hughes. My nanny Carina Valencia went to Halverton today to purchase a digital camera and groceries. Why have you detained her?"

"I'll be. She has been telling the truth."

"And what made you think otherwise?" Brock asked in his military voice.

"Well…you see…they say…"

"Who says?" He dropped his voice an octave and growled the question.

"The store clerks saw her run to the cart and act like she was going to take the baby. The mother screamed and Jason grabbed your nanny and waited for me to show up." As he recounted the incident, his confidence came back.

"Did you ask Ms. Valencia why she was "supposedly" taking the baby?"

"She said it looked like the mother was going to smother the baby, and she was just trying to help."

He relaxed, realizing it had all been a mistake. "That sounds like Ms. Valencia. She would never harm a child."

The back door banged, and he knew Maddie had come in to see what took him so long. "Release Ms. Valencia and let her get home before the storm hits."

"I can't."

"Why can't you?" Brock yelled in the phone.

"I can't find the mother to get her account of the

situation."

"Then you don't have any reason to hold her if there haven't been any charges against her. Officer Warren, let her go, or I'll sue your department starting with you."

He heard a squeak on the other end before the phone clicked.

"What's wrong with Carina?" The worry in his daughter's voice did nothing to quiet the worry swirling in his belly.

"I'm not sure. But if she isn't back by dinner, we'll make a trip to Halverton tonight."

Fifteen

The drive back to the ranch was the most exhausting trip she'd ever taken. It didn't help the weather turned nasty the last half hour.

Carina squinted through the snow flurries, trying to stay in the middle of the road. What would Brock say when she returned to the house? When Officer Warren walked into the room and told her Brock had vouched for her, she about fell out of the chair. How did she explain her behavior without telling him she killed her daughter?

The glowing light in the windows welcomed and terrified. She wanted to never stray from the ranch again. The drive was harrowing and then being treated like a criminal…but facing Brock and telling him the truth had to be worse than spending time in jail.

The headlights shone across the front windows when she parked. The door flew open and Maddie ran down the steps meeting her at the door of the truck. "You're finally back. We were starting to get worried."

"The roads were pretty bad. I had to go slow." She

motioned to the bags sitting on the seat. "Grab a couple of those and we'll only have to make one trip."

Maddie ran around to the passenger side and hugged two grocery sacks to her. Brock appeared as Carina took hold of two herself.

"We need to talk when the kids go to bed," he said, leaning past her to grab the last bags.

Carina swallowed and hurried into the house. Maybe purchasing a camera wasn't necessary. He could just kick her out for being arrested. Did he know what for? Probably. Officer Warren wasn't about to withhold that kind of information.

Thankfully, Maddie chattered about their day and what they did. Her cheerful conversation made putting the groceries away with Brock's steady gaze on her a little less disconcerting.

"Maddie, take Tate and get ready for bed. I'll be up shortly," Brock said, never taking his eyes from Carina.

She rubbed her hands up and down her arms. The room had become cold. Or was it just her nerves?

"Carina, will you read me a story?" Maddie's questioning eyes asked more than for a story. She could see the child witnessed her agitation.

"Yes, I'll be up after I have a cup of tea. The drive was nerve-wracking and I can't seem to get warm."

Maddie smiled, tucked Tate on her hip, and headed up the stairs.

Carina hurried to the stove with a kettle full of water. She was chilled to the bone.

"What was that all about today?" Brock asked, pushing his coffee cup to the middle of the table and standing.

"What was what all about?" She couldn't deny

being brought in by the police, but maybe, just maybe she wouldn't have to tell him everything.

"Dammit, Carina! You know what I'm talking about. I don't like getting calls from Johnson gloating and hoping I'm in jail." He crossed the room and grabbed her shoulders. "Why did you get hauled to the police station?"

"Oh, that. It was merely a misunderstanding." She turned to put a teabag in her cup.

"People don't get hauled to jail on misunderstandings."

"They do all the time in Chicago. It takes a while to sort things out sometimes." She crossed her arms and leaned against the counter to put space between them.

"Hae you been arrested before?" The shock on his face made her reach out to him.

"No! I've never been arrested before."

"I didn't think the nanny service would send us a felon, but damn, I need answers. You are the caretaker of my children. I won't lose them or the ranch to Johnson or anyone because of you."

That was it. He felt she jeopardized his life.

"I told you it was a misunderstanding. I overreacted when I heard a child in distress and the young mother overreacted to my help." She swallowed. His brown eyes stared at her revealing no emotion.

When he didn't say anything, she darted around him. "I'll read to Maddie now."

"What about your tea?"

"I'll get it later."

***

In the morning Brock didn't say a word at breakfast, but Carina felt him watching her.

"I'll be busy today. We've got some fence to fix on the far end." He swallowed the last of his coffee and stood.

"Do you want me to throw some sandwiches in a bag?"

"No. I'll come in at noon. I'll need to load some more hay."

"Do you have a list of the furniture you want to sell?" *That is if you still want to keep me around.*

"Yeah, it's sitting on the desk."

She listened to him put on his boots and coat. He hadn't made any more mention of her arrest or her being unfit for his children. But his distance chilled her.

Maddie was already on the computer in the office. Carina picked up the list of furniture and ruffled the girl's hair. She checked on Tate playing quietly in his playpen in the living room. Sitting on the couch, she read the list. His choices were good. She could see the pieces he chose bringing good money, yet not interrupting the family routine. She pulled the camera out of the bag, popped in the batteries, and wandered about the house.

Carina snapped the camera, knowing exactly who her mother would send the photos to first. She took several shots of each piece trying to get the best quality and show the lines of the furniture with limited light.

When the results satisfied her, she sat down at the computer. Using Maddie's e-mail to send the photos to her mom, she added a brief note about why they needed buyers and top dollar.

Now her mother would have another link to her. She shook her head. Couldn't be helped—this was business. Brock needed money.

Brock arrived at noon, downed soup and sandwiches, and headed back out to feed and continue checking the cattle.

Maddie begged to ride, so Carina bundled up Tate and they all spent the afternoon in the arena. Maddie rode and Carina wished she could be on a horse beside the girl.

"Could you at least let me brush your horse and lead it around?" Carina asked when Maddie finished riding and led her horse to the tack room.

Maddie smiled. "I don't think Daddy would get mad at that. Here." She handed Cookie to Carina.

She stroked the animal's soft nose and let the warm breath puff on her cheek. The thrill of holding the animal and running a hand over its strong sleek neck shocked her.

"Horses are magnificent animals," she said to no one in particular.

"I like them." Maddie watched her earnestly. "They're better than most people."

Carina hid her snicker and asked, "Why do you say that?"

"A horse is always happy to see you, and they don't boss you around." Maddie loosened the cinch and pulled the saddle from her mount.

"That's true. I would imagine you could tell things to a horse you can't tell anyone else. After all, who are they going to tell?" Carina joked, until she saw the surprised look on Maddie's face.

"How'd you know?" she whispered.

"Know what?"

"That I tell Cookie things I don't tell anyone else." She put the saddle on the rack and returned with a brush. She handed it to Carina.

"I didn't know you did exactly, but it makes sense to me. Everyone wants someone they can talk to who doesn't judge or repeat what they said." Carina brushed the horse. "An animal is the perfect friend for that reason."

Maddie smiled. "Yeah, like Daddy always talking to Roscoe. If that dog could talk, we'd know more of what Daddy thinks and could help him when he's sad."

Carina turned to Maddie. "So that's who your Daddy confides in." She leaned down and whispered, "I thought maybe he spent so much time with the cows he lectured them."

Maddie went into a fit of giggles.

"Put your horse up, I'm going in to make dinner," Carina said, picking up Tate and motioning for Maddie to put the horse away.

Less than half an hour later, Carina handed Tate a peeled carrot when heavy steps on the back porch followed by a knock startled Carina. They didn't get company much and the footsteps weren't Brock or Willie T. She wiped her hands on her apron and made her way to the back door.

Jack stood on the porch holding his hat in his hands. "Brock wanted me to tell you not to wait dinner for him. He's got a cow having a hard birth. He'll be in when the calf's on the ground."

Disappointment took hold before she realized his being out late would keep her from having to endure another awkward meal.

"Thank you, Jack. Are you sure he's going to be okay out there by himself?" Clouds had been steadily gathering all afternoon, bringing dusk earlier than usual.

"He'll be fine. I saw Maddie in the barn and told her." Jack plopped his hat on his head and turned to leave.

Maddie ran out of the darkness. "I'm starving. Can we eat now, since Jack says Daddy won't be home for a while?"

Carina smiled at the child. "Doesn't it bother you when your father is out late?"

"No. He knows what he's doing." Maddie washed her hands at the sink in the mud room. "And I know mommy watches over him."

Carina closed her eyes. *Who watches over me?*

"Are you okay?" Maddie asked.

Carina opened her eyes and smiled. "I'm fine. Wash up for dinner and get your brother, please."

***

When the kids were in bed, Carina took a bath. After soaking until the water was tepid, she pulled on her night slip and wrapped up in a thick robe. She sat in the living room reading a horse book waiting for Brock. As the clock chimed ten, she heard a noise at the front of the house. Her gaze shot to the door with only a small hook for a latch. It wouldn't keep anyone out.

Sitting straight up in the chair, fear prickled her skin. She hadn't locked the back door knowing Brock would be coming home. The sound of footsteps on the front porch sent a chill down her spine. Who would be here this time of night? Jack went home, Willie T always entered through the back door. She pulled the robe tight around her and stood. She had to see who was out there and protect the children.

Walking quietly across the cold wood floor, she

took comfort from the wool rug in front of the door. Digging her toes into the pile of the mat, she pulled the curtain back only enough for her to peer down the length of the porch.

A man stood at the end of the porch. His silhouette showed a paunchy belly. It wasn't anyone she knew. Carina slipped the hook out of the latch.

"May I help you?" she asked, opening the door only enough to show her face.

The man started, then walked toward her. He squinted in the dark, as if trying to get a good look at her.

"You the whore Brock has living here?" The man's contemptuous voice and comment sent her from guarded to angry.

"I *am not* a whore. I am the children's nanny as if that is any business of yours, Mr.—"

"Johnson."

She should have known by his attitude.

"Brock isn't here. So you may as well leave yourself." She pushed her weight against the door when he attempted to push it open.

"You aren't being too hospitable."

"Mostly because you aren't welcome here. Especially at this time of night."

"I came to throw some numbers at Brock. Show him how much he has to gain by selling this dump." He pushed at the door and craned his neck. Carina knew he tried to get a look at her, and she wasn't about to let this man see her or set foot in the house.

"He isn't interested. This ranch isn't for sale."

"How does a *nanny* know this? You seem to be awful cozy for just working with the kids." The accusation in his voice turned her anger up another notch.

"Mr. Johnson, only people with their minds in the gutter would think the things you seem to be indicating. Now, please leave, and I'll let Brock know you were here." With one last effort, she put her back against the door and pushed with her legs, closing out the man. Sliding the hook into the eye, she smiled with satisfaction.

He uttered foul words she hoped didn't drift up to Maddie's window. Listening closely, she heard an engine start up and drive off. Why hadn't she heard him arrive? If Roscoe had been there, he would have sounded the alarm when the car approached. Maybe they needed two dogs; Roscoe, to help with the cows, and one to stay and guard the house.

Agitated by the man's rudeness, Carina entered the kitchen and made herself a cup of hot chocolate. Settling on the couch in the living room, she sipped the beverage and drifted off to sleep.

***

Brock's bones ached with fatigue. Between the heater blasting to thaw out his limbs and the fatigue from pulling the calf, it was a wonder he arrived home and hadn't ended up in a bar pit asleep. He spotted the light on in the mudroom when he pulled up to the house. His heart raced thinking Carina waited for him.

Entering the house, he didn't hear a sound. If she had been awake, she would have heard the pickup with its rumbling muffler and met him at the door. Or so he'd dreamed all the way home.

He peeled off his dirty, cold clothes, and stepped into the small bathroom. Turning on the shower to heat the water, he looked at his tired face in the mirror. He needed a shave and a haircut. He looked like an old hippie. But right now was not the time to make a trip to the barber in Halverton.

He stepped into the shower. The hot water stung, pelting his cold body. Lathering up, he wondered about Carina's arrest. She wasn't telling him something. He saw it in the fear in her eyes. What could be in her past that haunted her? They had to keep after this month. They all needed her.

Did she get all the photos taken today? She seemed to know a lot about antiques, but could he really get enough out of a few pieces of furniture to pay her wages?

He wanted her stay here legitimate. With his ex-father-in-law starting rumors in Halverton, it would be hard enough to keep people from thinking poorly of Carina and himself.

The water started to cool. He turned off the faucet and stepped out of the shower, toweling off. Wrapping the towel around his waist, he headed for the stairs.

"No! Don't take her!" Carina's shouts from the living room set his heart racing.

He looked around and spotted her sitting up on the couch. Hurrying over, he sat down beside her. When he raised his hand to push the hair out of her face, she pulled back, fear lighting her eyes and contorting her face.

"No, I didn't mean to." Her hand and arms raised, whether to ward off a blow or grab something, he couldn't tell.

Brock grasped her shoulders and shook her. "Carina, honey. It's me, Brock. Wake up." She attempted to fight him. Her robe slid down her shoulders, bunching above his hands. The sight of her creamy shoulders and long throat caused his groin to come to life.

"Shh." He pulled her tight against his chest, holding her. Her body sagged against him and sobs wracked her body.

"No one's going to hurt you. I'm here." He crooned as he smoothed her soft hair and breathed in her sweet, floral scent. When her crying abated, he continued to hold her.

"What didn't you mean to do?" he asked and felt her stiffen. "These dreams aren't manifestations, they come from something real."

She tried to pull out of his embrace, but he wasn't ready to let her go.

"Is this something to do with your arrest?"

Her head nodded, rubbing on his bare chest. Brock ground his teeth to keep his groin from exploding. It had been a long time since he'd been naked and held a woman. The skin-to-skin contact and her soft curves in his arms just about took him over the brink of sanity. But he had to keep a level head and discover his nanny's secret.

Sixteen

"What happened?" Brock put a finger under her chin, lifting her face to his. Tears clung to her dark lashes.

Wiping at the tears, Carina sniffed. Swallowing hard, her lips trembled. "I lost a child."

Her eyes sought his and his gut reaction was sorrow for her and the child. "If only I'd—" She shivered. Brock gathered her into his arms.

"If only you'd what?" He ran his hand up and down her back, feeling the soft skin and silky fabric under his rough hands.

"Listened to Perry." She pushed out of his arms. "I can't stay here. You shouldn't have someone watching your children who killed her own." When she started to stand Brock pulled her back down into his lap.

"You didn't kill your child."

"You don't understand." She flailed her arms and legs trying to break loose.

He held on even as his exhausted body cramped. "No, I don't understand. Tell me how a woman as devoted and loving as you could kill a child."

She stopped struggling and turned in his arms. Placing her hands on either side of his face, she stared into his eyes. "I-I went to help my mom move furniture. Perry told me not to. He worried the whole time I was pregnant. But he didn't want a child. He wanted an ornament to look good with his CEO who believed a family man worked harder." She gulped. Her body shook, "But I didn't listen to him and my baby. She came too early. I killed her."

Brock's heart stopped. He saw the horror of the moment in her blue eyes. He pulled her to him. "You didn't harm your baby."

She pushed away from him. "It was my fault! No one else. I killed her." Tears trickled down her cheeks. "Brock, I can't stay here. What if I do something to harm your children? I have to leave."

"No. You don't. I know you would never harm my children. Just like you didn't intentionally harm your baby." Brock couldn't deny the fear and sorrow in her eyes.

"I can feel it here." She pounded on her chest. "I died in here. And Perry left me. His last words were, 'You lost the baby just to bring him down.'"

Brock took her head in his hands and kissed the tears on her cheeks. Tasting the saltiness of her pain and breathing the scent of her sweet skin, he knew he'd do whatever it took to make her believe that she didn't kill her child. Lowering his lips to hers, all he wanted to do was chase away her fears.

Relief seeped out of Carina at telling Brock. When he kissed her, the whole world seemed right. As if her past no longer existed. Winding her hands in his long hair, she found it wet, and his body naked. The hard bulge between him and her thigh sent a shiver of longing throughout her body.

Her robe slid the rest of the way down her shoulders, pooling in his lap. His hand left the heated path it made down her arm long enough to flip off the lamp.

In the darkness, he slipped her night clothes over her head, leaving her naked in his lap. Only the thin barrier of her robe on his lap separated them. As his hands grasped her breasts, she moaned softly. He pulled her back against his hard body. His tongue made a wet trail down her neck to her shoulder. She leaned against him, reaching up behind her to draw his lips down to hers.

His hands continued to mold her breasts before gliding down her torso to the pulsing spot between her legs. When his fingers whispered down the inside of her thighs, she wiggled and sighed as heat coursed through her. The magic of his hands had her pressing closer, wishing for more.

Sliding his hands under her bottom, he helped her stand. The robe slithered by her legs as he turned her to face him. His warm, wet mouth sought her nipples while his hands spread her legs and drew her down onto his lap.

His firmness brushed against her throbbing center as she knelt on the couch straddling his lap. Taking him in her hands, her body surged anew. His firmness and length aroused her. Feeling the velvety softness of his arousal, she wanted him. Wanted to give herself to him completely. She ached to have him fill her and feel the love of a good man. If only once in her lifetime.

Without waiting for a sign from him, she shifted, placing her body over his shaft and lowering slowly, enjoying the moans and heavy breathing of the man under her. When it felt as if the tip would touch her heart, he began moving in smooth, unhurried motions.

Carina flung her head back, gyrating against his motions and panting. The sensations rocked her senses, exploding lights in her head, culminating in blackness before the sensations started all over again. Brock grasped her nipples, rolling them between his fingers. The simple act along with his rhythmic thrusting spiraled all feeling to her center. Whispering his name on a whoosh of air, she collapsed to his chest.

When the sparklers in her head dimmed and she could speak, Carina shoved away from his chest to look into his face. "I've never… Oh my."

Brock grinned and kissed her. "Me either." He hugged her tight, enjoying the feel of her breasts pressed against his chest and her body wrapped around him. Making love to her filled the emptiness he'd harbored since Cindy left. What he felt for Carina wasn't the simplistic love of childhood, nor the animalistic lust he had for Cindy. No. The woman in his arms warmed him for the way she loved his children, relished life for the simple things, and her bravery. How many women would leave everything they knew and loved to start a new life?

He heard the upstairs toilet flush. "I'm enjoying holding you, but we better get you dressed and off to your room before Maddie decides to do a bed check."

"Oh. I forgot about the children." The distress in her voice endeared her even more.

"Shh. I'll wrap this towel around and head up like I

just came out of the shower down here." He lifted Carina off his lap, groaning as he slipped from her body. Having her wrapped around him created contentment he wanted to relive again, and soon.

Small footsteps sounded in the upstairs hall. "Are you okay?" he whispered, wrapping the towel around him, hoping the coolness of the wet towel and the sight of his daughter would shrink the appendage holding the towel at a point. Brock scanned the length of Carina's naked body and knew having tasted her gifts he would have trouble keeping his hands to himself in the morning.

"Hurry before she comes down," Carina said, digging around on the couch for her nightie.

"Just put your robe on and slip into my room when you come up," he said, smiling and heading for the stairs.

"I'll not have Maddie catch me slipping into or out of your room."

"I was afraid of that."

Brock disappeared up the stairs. Carina sat on the couch listening. She could hear Brock's deep voice and then Maddie's young voice. Their footsteps moved to the girl's bedroom. After a few minutes, Brock's heavy footsteps padded down the hall to his room.

She found her night slip slung across the farthest arm of the couch and slid it over her head. As the material skimmed across her sensitive nipples, a rush of heat seared her body. Passion rippled down low in her torso, rekindling the fire Brock had detonated.

Sliding her arms into her robe, she pulled it tight around her. Now that she knew the security of his arms and the passion of his kisses, how was she to leave? She couldn't be his nanny indefinitely. After telling him about losing her child, there was no way a family man like himself would even think of becoming attached to a woman like her.

Climbing the stairs, she hugged her arms around her. What was she to do now? At the top stair, she listened and looked toward Maddie's door. Not a sound came from the room and light didn't glow under the child's door. Her two greatest fears were that Brock would not trust her with his children knowing her past, and Maddie would find Carina sleeping with her father.

Carina tiptoed down the hall to her room and opened the door quietly. The latch barely clicked when she shut the door. Crossing the room to her bed, she untied the robe and slid it down her arms, tossing it across the footboard.

Something moved on the bed. Her heart thudded in her chest. She scanned the shadows at the head of bed.

"What are you doing in here?" she hissed.

"I wanted you to fall asleep in my arms."

She could just make out Brock's eyebrows wiggling as he threw back the covers revealing his naked body and open arms.

"We can't do this. Not with Maddie just across the hall."

"She'll fall deep asleep now that she knows I'm home safe." He waved her forward with his hands.

Carina hovered at the edge of the bed. She didn't want to give in. She knew what they'd done in the living room was unacceptable, but had been unavoidable. She'd tried to ignore her attraction to Brock since the day she stepped onto his front porch.

"Brock, spending the night in your arms might

chase away my dreams, but it doesn't change the facts." When he didn't respond, she continued, "You could decide at any time to toss me." She motioned from her to him. "This would just complicate things. Not the least, what if Maddie finds out."

"Marry me."

Carina gaped at him. He couldn't possibly mean what he'd just said. He was against marriage.

She looked around for his towel and found his tightie whities instead. Picking them up off the floor, she tossed them to him. "Don't say that unless you mean it." She held up a hand when he started to speak. "I won't marry just so you can have me in your bed."

Brock sat up. "You're good for this family."

Carina walked to the head of the bed and brushed his hair off his forehead. "I've become fond of your children and their father, but I can't. You don't want someone like me."

Brock wound his arms around her, pulling her down onto the bed. "How do you know what I want?" He kissed her neck and started up her jaw. Shivers of delight tingled her senses.

"You want a farm woman. Someone who can help you with the cows and give you more children." She turned, avoiding his lips. She wanted to taste him again, but to give in to one kiss would melt her defenses.

"I want you." With that bold statement, he captured her mouth with his.

She lost.

His quick hands striped her night slip over her head and elicited pleasure over her body before she had a chance to object—or wonder how he planned to steal out of the room in the morning without Maddie being the wiser.

***

Brock woke with his arms wrapped around Carina. Her body molded to his nicely. Her bottom tucked against his groin had already brought him to life. Glancing at the clock, he groaned. There wasn't going to be any hanky-panky this morning. He had to get out of this room before Maddie stirred.

Easing his arm out from under Carina, he felt her move. If she woke up, he'd be tempted to linger in bed. It was a wonderful thought, but not a wise one. Sliding across the bed, he dropped his legs over the edge and picked up his shorts.

When his shorts were on, he left the room, quietly walking down the hall to the bathroom. Once inside he breathed a sigh of relief. Maddie wouldn't think anything of seeing him come out of this room. He stared at his reflection in the mirror. Flashes of conversation from the previous night were disjointed between explicit reminders of the effect of Carina's body against his.

Marry me. He started. Had he really asked her to marry him? Pulling the shaving cream out of the cabinet, he piled a white mound in his hand and stared at it. He didn't remember her jumping in his arms and shouting, 'yes'. That was a good thing.

But then after what they did last night, it would be caddish of him not to marry her. His hand shook as he reached for his razor. What if she became pregnant? They hadn't used anything. Was that why she didn't want to marry? She was afraid she'd lose another child. He thunked himself in the head and splattered shaving cream all over the mirror.

Of course, that was why she didn't want to marry. She believed she couldn't bring a healthy child into the world.

He'd been thinking with his cock and not his head. *Damn!* That was the cause of his disastrous marriage to Cindy. But she didn't like kids. Carina adored Maddie and Tate. If nothing else, marrying her would give the kids what they needed. He smiled. And some good romps in bed for him.

He shook his head. She deserved more from a marriage than that. She deserved a man who loved her.

***

While in his room dressing, Brock decided to wait and see if Carina brought up his proposal. When he arrived in the kitchen, Maddie already had coffee brewing and bacon frying.

"Carina's slow this morning," she said, not looking up from her task of cracking eggs.

"Maybe she waited up for me last night," he replied, hoping guilt didn't show in his words.

"She did. I'm surprised you didn't see her." The vague comment jerked his head around. Did she know about their romp on the couch?

"She must have gone to bed before I got here."

"Must have." Maddie stared at him. The censure in her eyes just about knocked him to his knees. She knew.

"Maddie…"

"Daddy, don't lie to me." She tossed an empty eggshell on the counter and turned to him. "I know you and Carina like each other." Her face turned red. "And I know that you slept with her last night."

When he started to open his mouth, she held her

hand up. "I don't care. If she makes you and this family happy, I don't care what people say." She pointed a finger at him. "But don't lie to me. Cindy lied to me all the time. You started doing it, too, until she left. Don't start it again. I'm old enough now to know the truth."

"Freckles, I only lied when Cindy was here to save your feelings."

"Well, I'm big enough now you don't have to save my feelings. I like Carina. And if you don't ask her to marry you…I'll…well, I'll think of something."

Brock pulled Maddie into his arms, embracing her and kissing the top of her head. "I already asked her and she refused." The more he thought about her refusal, the more he wondered at her reasons.

Maddie pulled out of his embrace. "Why? Because of us kids?"

"No." Carina's answer startled both of them.

"How long have you been standing there?" he asked, straightening and walking toward the woman who'd captured his daughter and given him the gift of a passion-filled night.

"Long enough." She patted his arm and moved past him to stop in front of Maddie. "Honey, I told your father no, because," she peered at him as if he had the answer, "I don't belong here."

"What do you mean you don't belong here?" Brock's anger grew at her insistence she knew better than him.

"I grew up in the city. I'm only here for a while. Just to get my life back in order after…you know." She turned to him, asking with her eyes not to tell Maddie.

"A miscarriage isn't your fault." He thought she was going to hit him. Her hands fisted and her face reddened.

"Carina, I'm sorry." Maddie threw her arms around the woman.

Wiping at the tears trickling down her cheeks, Carina stared daggers at him. "I don't want sympathy. If I wanted that I'd have stayed in Chicago with my smothering mother and cloying friends."

"You need to realize it wasn't your fault." Brock poured a cup of coffee and sat at the table.

"I'd rather not talk about this right now." Carina moved about the kitchen finishing the breakfast Maddie had started.

Brock stood and crossed the room to place a hand on Carina's arm. If Maddie knew they slept together, then he didn't need to restrain himself from touching Carina. She may have refused to marry him, which he had to admit stung a little even though it also relieved him, but she couldn't deny the passion that flared between them. When Carina looked at him, he tipped her face up and kissed her full on the lips. She started to pull away, and he wrapped an arm around her waist, holding her close.

"We aren't going to let you walk out of our lives without a fight," he said, tilting his head toward Maddie. Carina's eyes widened and her body relaxed.

"We can't..." she pushed against him as she protested.

He held firm and kissed her again until she relaxed in his arms. "You're not running anymore. Get that furniture sold. I have a payment to make until I can make you come to your senses and marry me."

She glanced at Maddie and back at him. "You shouldn't talk like that in front of Maddie."

"Why not? There aren't going to be any secrets in this house."

"I don't have any secrets. Not anymore." She pulled out of his arms this time and walked over to the sink.

Brock walked up behind her. The pink sky and orange orb of the sun painted the world outside the window in vibrant color.

"Without secrets, we can confront all our fears."

She peered at him from over her shoulder. "Your fears are more valid than mine. You can battle them." She sighed and hung her head. "Mine are all in my head."

"Stay and let us help you slay them." He wrapped his arms around her shoulders, and they watched the sun rise into the sky, bringing the snow-covered ground to sparkling life.

Carina wanted to feel his strong arms around her and the warmth of his breath on her neck every day. To be a part of this family and loved by every one of them would be blissful. She'd yet to hear Brock say those three little words. Until she did, she would not jeopardize her heart.

Seventeen

Roscoe started barking and Maddie ran to the back door. "Willie T's here," she called, slamming the door and running out to greet him.

Brock continued to hold Carina as they watched Maddie and Willie T put their heads together before entering the house.

"She's telling him everything she thinks she knows," he said, giving Carina a slight squeeze before stepping away to pull a cup out of the cupboard. Handing the cup to Carina, who reached for the coffee pot, he added, "You may remain at Haven as long as you want, married or not." He stared into her eyes wanting her to know his proposal the night before wasn't being taken back this morning.

Stomping and giggles echoed in the mudroom before Willie T and Maddie entered the kitchen.

"Is that breakfast I smell?" the old man asked, sitting down in his usual spot at the kitchen table. Brock placed the cup of coffee in front of him and motioned for Carina to take a seat as well.

She poured two more cups of coffee and placed one in front of Brock before sitting to his right.

The phone rang. Carina exchanged pleasantries with Willie T when Brock went to answer the phone. Who would call this early in the morning?

She swirled the coffee in her cup barely registering Brock said her name as she contemplated how to get out of the mess she'd made.

"Carina. It's for you." He held the phone out toward her. Did she give Georgie this number?

"Who is it?"

Brock smiled, "Your mother."

Her mother? She thought of Brock's proposal. Talking to her mother would remind her of all she'd left behind and would have to return to.

Carina gripped the phone in both hands. "Mom?"

"Yes, Carina."

Tears warmed her eyes hearing the familiar, loving voice. Even though she came all this way to put distance between them, until the miscarriage, they had been very close.

"Don't cry," her mother said, in a voice on the verge of doing the same.

"How did you know?"

"What?"

"That I was crying?" Carina brushed at the tears. The three at the table had their heads bowed together as if talking.

"Because you never could keep emotion out of your voice. How do you think I always knew you were in mischief?"

"It's so good to hear you."

"Are you sure? I thought you moved way out west

to get away from me." The pout in her mother's voice filled her with guilt, but no regrets.

"I miss you, too, but this move has been good for me. Did you get the photos I e-mailed?"

"Yes, they're wonderful pieces. In fact, Mrs. Thomlin may purchase all of them for her summer cottage at the lake."

Carina pumped her hand in the air. She knew they would catch the eye of someone who'd pay top dollar. "When she does, e-mail me and I'll give you the name and address of where to send the money."

Brock's head popped up. "Just have her put it in your bank account. I assume she has access?"

"It will be more than my wages," she said, holding the phone away from her ear. "And it needs to go to the nanny agency."

"How do you know it will be more?" His dark eyes glowed with stubbornness.

"We'll discuss this later," she said, turning her attention back to the phone.

"What was that all about?" her mother asked in an amused tone.

"I'll tell you later. When you sell the pieces put the money in my account."

"But I thought these belonged to the family you work for?"

"They do. Mom, it's a long, complicated story. Just put the money in my account."

"You haven't turned to stealing or something?"

"Mother! No. Just do as I ask."

"Are you taking care of yourself? You know after a trauma like yours it sometimes…"

"I'm fine, Mother. Give me a call when you put the

money in." Carina didn't want to hear all about how she should be taking care of herself.

"I love you, Mom. Bye." Carina hung up the phone but kept her hand on the receiver. They'd always been close. The year since the miscarriage had pushed them apart. Her mother had never dealt well with loss. First her husband and then her granddaughter. Carina pinched the bridge of her nose. Loss wasn't easy on anyone.

An arm circled her shoulder, and she looked up into Brock's concerned eyes.

"She'll be fine." The calmness of his voice made her trust him to be right.

She turned, wrapping her arms around his middle and burying her face in his strong chest. "I know she will, it's me I'm worried about," she whispered, clinging to his strength. How had she gone this long holding all the guilt in? Having spilled her secret, it was as if someone pulled the plug and she was swirling down the drain. Everything was out of her control, and she had no idea where it would lead.

Eighteen

Carina sat atop a brown mare with a calm disposition and slow gait. "I know you're afraid something bad could happen, but putting me on a horse that's about to croak isn't going to teach me how to ride," she said to Brock's back as his horse briskly outdistanced her.

"Copper isn't about to keel over. She's a wise twenty-seven and a good teacher for someone who's never been on a horse." The glint in his eye when he turned his horse to come back to her slow-moving stead, told her he was up to something.

"You took an hour teaching me all about the tack and how to put them on and what could be wrong if a horse starts acting up when they are saddled and bridled. I want to run around the arena like Maddie and Cookie." With that, she nudged her horse in the ribs. Surprisingly, the mare shot forward, forcing Carina to sit back hard in the saddle. She grabbed the horn with both hands. The rhythm of the animal bounced her up and down like a midget dribbling a basketball.

"Whoa, whoa!" she shouted, but the beast kept on bouncing, causing her breasts to ache and her butt to throb. Realizing she wasn't going to fall off, she let loose of the horn to stabilize her bouncing body parts.

A shrill whistle brought Copper to a stop so fast Carina had to put her hands out to keep from falling over the horse's shoulder. Thundering hooves echoed in the building. Brock rode his horse up alongside.

"What was that about?" The anger in his eyes softened when his gaze traveled down her arms to her clutched bosom. "Do you own any bras beside the flimsy one you had on the other day?"

Her cheeks heated at the mention of their interrupted heavy petting in the barn. After all, they were alone in the barn once more, and she'd thought of that day many times while slowly walking the mare around the arena.

"One."

"Well, next time you ride, wear it. A woman needs to support her breasts when she rides. That's why I had you only walk."

"I don't believe you. You had me walk so I wouldn't want to ride again." His eyebrow shot up. She'd hit the reason he'd made everything about riding boring. "Admit it. You made this first lesson intentionally boring, so I wouldn't hound you to give me more."

"I wasn't boring you intentionally." He reached out. "Let me help." His horse moved next to hers and his hands gently massaged her sore breasts. The heat his touch generated whisked away any trace of irritation the trotting horse caused.

She stood up in the stirrups and twisted. "Um, it

hurts here, too." She pointed to her right buttocks, and he grinned, placing a hand on her bruised body part.

"Mmmm." His hands made more than her sore bottom heat.

"I'm trained in massage therapy," he whispered before his lips brushed her ear.

"Really?"

"I can show you. In the feed stall." He dismounted, leading his horse and hers across the arena.

"It's the middle of the day, what about the kids?" she asked, glancing around, wondering how a riding lesson could turn into a mid-afternoon tryst. Knowing if she went through with it, she'd lose more of her heart to a man who didn't want a commitment. Sure, he'd asked her to marry him, but it was only a ruse to keep her here for the children. She knew that. He'd yet to utter the words that would make her stay.

"Willie T will keep them busy." He reached up to help her off the horse. He held her in the air, her feet dangling, kissing her until she forgot everything, but the wonderful sensations his kiss spread through her body. She slid down his chest, her wobbly legs barely held her when he tucked her against his side and escorted her to the familiar pile of hay.

"We really shouldn't. Not here, where anyone can walk in on us." Even as she uttered the words, her hands worked the snaps on his jacket free. She knew each time she made love with Brock would make it harder to leave, but she couldn't stop. It was more than the need to feel his strong arms around her. She wanted to make him forget Beth and see her for someone he could someday love.

"Who could walk in? Willie T has the kids. Jack is

out with the cows." He unzipped her coat, pushing it off her arms. Heat rippled in her belly as his hands slid under her shirt, cupping her tender breasts. For a moment, all thoughts left her. His touch spiraled heat through her body. Shaking her head, she knew there was something… She sighed when his mouth covered hers. Fighting the desire to succumb to his touch, her mind wrestled to capture a piece of information she knew was important. Something that should have been mentioned…

She went still, remembering the visitor the night before. Dragging her lips from his, she said, "Beth's dad."

Brock's body went rigid, putting space between them. His hands stopped their exploration. "What?"

"Mr. Johnson could show up."

"Why would he come out here?" His eyes didn't hold the heat of passion anymore. They darkened with indignation.

Carina stepped back. Brock's hands fell to his side and bunched in fists. "With everything that happened, I forgot to tell you he was here last night. Before you got back from checking the cows." She reached down for her coat. Brock grabbed it from her, helping her back into it.

"What did he want?"

"He said something about talking some numbers over with you. But I think he mainly just wanted to get a look at me." Anger flared at the memory of his words. "He called me a whore. He doesn't even know me."

Brock uttered a string of profanity and snapped his coat shut. "That son-of-a-bitch has no right on this property or calling you names."

"Where are you going?" Fear for Brock had her clinging to his arm as he started out of the stall.

"To call him and tell him to keep the hell off my land."

Carina let him go. His anger wasn't consolable. She gathered the horses and led them to the tack room. After unsaddling and brushing the animals, she put them out and headed to the house.

Brock stormed out of the house as her foot touched the bottom porch step. He didn't even acknowledge her when he passed. Not wishing to take the brunt of his anger, she let him go as Roscoe hurried around the side of the house.

Stomping to his pickup, Brock mumbled under his breath and wondered not for the first time, why the hell he let the man get to him. No one could make him sell the ranch, so why did he resent the man trying?

Because the son-of-a-bitch knew how much the land meant to him.

Selling the ranch would be the equivalent of selling Maddie or Tate. It was a part of him. He loved it.

Jamming the vehicle in gear, he slammed his foot on the accelerator. The pickup roared to life, fishtailing out of the yard and onto the road. He'd find Jack, check on the cows, and make a trip around the perimeter of the property.

It would give him a chance to make sure Mr. Johnson hadn't brought people out to inspect the land, hoping someone would offer an amount Brock couldn't refuse.

He slammed his palm on the steering wheel. He'd never sell. Now that Carina was here, Maddie would return to school after the Christmas break and things would get back to normal.

But how long would Carina stay? He rubbed his gut. The thought of her leaving was something he didn't want to think about. But it was inevitable. After a while, she'd want to return to Chicago and her family and friends. All city women slowly began to crave what they left behind.

A pain shot through his head. He had to find a way to make her stay. The kids needed her. *He needed her*.

Jack's pickup sat on the side of the road not far from the first feed bunk. Brock stopped. Squinting at the sun's glare on the snow, he peered among the huddle of cows eating hay. There wasn't a sign of Jack anywhere. The sun nearly touched the top of the Steens Mountains. Before long it would disappear behind the mountains, cloaking the valley in darkness.

The hair at the nape of his neck itched. Something wasn't right. He stepped out of the pickup—grabbing his rifle, flashlight, and a pair of gloves. Reaching out, he felt the hood of the Toyota. Cold.

Pulling on his gloves, he snapped the flashlight onto his belt loop and headed around the cows, looking for footprints in the snow. At the far side, he found a set of human tracks. He whistled for Roscoe and set out following the trail.

Peering back and forth between the footprints and the horizon, he walked for half an hour, fearing for his friend. The tracks appeared labored. Now and then he spotted a drop of blood. Finally, as the golden glow of sunlight faded to a washed-out yellow, Roscoe ran ahead of him barking.

Brock jogged in the direction of the noisy dog. Down in a gully, out of the wind, Jack knelt behind a young cow birthing a calf.

"Quiet Roscoe. Stay." Brock slid down into the gully and grabbed hold of one of the calf's legs. Together they pulled.

"I hoped someone would come looking for me. We've been at this several hours," Jack said between grunts.

Brock looked at the cow, she wasn't pushing anymore. The calf's head and body were out. It appeared the hips had hung up.

"We can't lose him, Jack," Brock said, thinking of his vulture of a father-in-law.

"I know. The calf seems to be alive, I just can't…"

"Pull more toward her feet," Brock said, slanting the calf down away from the cow's tail. He braced a foot against the cow's back end. "Ready. One. Two. Three."

Together they pulled, tugging back and forth, easing the hips out. When the calf slipped to the ground the cow gave a half-hearted call.

Dropping to his knees, Brock slapped the calf's side and slid his finger into its mouth to remove the mucous. When he felt the ribs moving, he dragged the newborn over to the mother's head. The cow licked and massaged the calf.

Both the mother and offspring had been stressed from the ordeal. When the calf raised his head, Brock was overwhelmed. The miracle unclenched a little of the fear he felt at possibly losing his family's home.

"I'll bring them some hay. You go home clean up and get a good night's sleep." Brock slapped the man beside him on the back. "Thank you."

"I know what every calf means to you and your

family. When I saw her walking around with the feet sticking out, I figured she was having problems."

Brock put an arm around Jack's shoulders. "Let's get back to the vehicles so you can get warmed up."

***

Carina walked back and forth in the kitchen. Darkness settled over the house hours ago and no sign or word from Brock.

"He's okay," Maddie said, pushing the green beans around her plate.

"Then why aren't you eating?" Having seen the fury on Brock's face when he left, she wasn't sure where he went or what he did. Maddie also witnessed the conversation and her father's angry departure. The child was as nervous and worried as Carina.

"I'm not eating because I'm not really hungry." Maddie pushed her plate to the middle of the table.

Carina bit her lip. She should have never mentioned Mr. Johnson's visit. He hadn't done anything. He went away when she told him to.

"May I be excused? I'm going to talk to Rayanne on the computer," Maddie said, interrupting her thoughts.

"Oh! Yes, go ahead. It will take your mind off your dad." Carina wiped Tate's face and lifted him out of the high chair. "I'm going to take Tate up and give him a bath."

Maddie waved her hand in acknowledgment and disappeared into the office.

Carina looked at the dirty dishes and food sitting on the table. The food had to be stored, but she'd take care of the dishes later. Setting Tate on the floor, she covered the food, stacking it in the refrigerator. When she turned to take Tate for his bath, he was gone.

"Tate, where are you?" she called, walking out of the kitchen and into the living room. Flicking on the lights as she went, Carina peered behind and under furniture. There wasn't any sign of the boy.

She hurried down the hall to the office. "Maddie, have you seen your brother?"

The girl pulled her attention away from the flickering computer screen. "Tate? No. Why?"

"I let him out of his high chair while I put the food away and he's disappeared."

Maddie's eyes grew round and worried. "First Daddy's missing and now Tate?"

The knot in Carina's stomach sunk deeper and heavier. She'd lost Tate. After confessing she killed her own child to Brock, what would he think when he came home and found his son missing?

Nineteen

Brock could barely keep his eyes open driving the last mile to the house. After feeding the rest of the cows and making sure the cow and calf were out of danger, he drove a quick perimeter check. He only found cattle tracks. The sight lessened his anger, but it still ate at him, Johnson had the nerve to confront Carina. No doubt he had called her names. The man was known for his nasty tongue.

He didn't think Johnson would trespass, but if he showed up at the house the night before- there was no telling what the man was thinking. Ever since Johnson's wife died, he'd become obsessed with pulling the ranch out from under Brock and the kids and taking Maddie.

Driving up to the house, it surprised him to see all the lights blazing. It was midnight. Everyone should be tucked in bed.

Before the motor died, the back door flew open. A frazzled Carina hurried down the steps.

"I can't find Tate." The anxiety in her voice shook

away his drowsiness.

"When did he disappear?" He took Carina by the arm, steering her back into the house.

"I set him on the floor while I cleaned up after dinner. When I turned around, he was gone." Tears trickled down her cheeks. "Maddie and I've looked everywhere." She turned to him. The anguish on her face tore at his heart. "I can't find him. First, I killed my child and now I've lost your son." She wailed. "I have to leave. I can't be around children."

He wrapped his arms around the woman, consoling her while his mind raced to all the places he'd hidden as a child.

"Did you try the space under the stairs?"

When she didn't respond, he shook her gently. "Carina, did you check the space under the stairs?"

"What space? Maddie helped me look she'd know about that wouldn't she?"

"Not really, Maddie isn't a hider." Brock released her, moving through the mudroom and down the hall. He pushed aside an old table to reveal a small triangular hole. Kneeling, he looked into the small recess under the stairs. Sure enough, there was Tate curled up sleeping soundly with his stuffed bull.

Brock reached into the space, pulling out his son. With Tate cradled in his arms, he stood.

Carina rushed to them. "How did you know that's where he was?" Relief softened her tense face.

"I was a boy once."

Carina reached out, gently brushing a blond curl off his son's forehead. The emotions on her face triggered feelings Brock thought would never cross his heart again.

"Why would he crawl in there and not come when we called him?" Fear and uncertainty flickered in her eyes. "Did I do something to upset him?"

"I'm sure it was just a matter of him crawling into the space and falling asleep," Brock said, mounting the stairs to put Tate in bed and distance himself from the woman who had crept into his heart with her tenderness and love of his children.

"I'll wake Maddie and send her to bed before I warm up some dinner for you," Carina said, moving to the sleeping child on the couch.

Only months before he would have fallen into bed exhausted and hungry, waiting till morning for breakfast. The woman who'd come into their lives was a blessing in more ways than one.

He placed Tate in his crib, bending to kiss his son's soft, plump cheek, before he raised the railing. His children were all he needed to get through this life. His heart fluttered. However, having someone caring and easy to be around like Carina made things simpler. No matter how much his body responded to her, he would not allow his mind to even think of a future with her. There were too many solid reasons to keep her out of his heart. One the fact she was a city woman who would return when the novelty of country life wore off.

His stomach growled, reminding him the woman in his thoughts was in the kitchen making him hot food. Closing the door gently behind him, he headed for Maddie's room. Sitting on the bed, he leaned down to kiss her.

"Daddy, it wasn't Carina's fault we couldn't find Tate." She sat up. "We were both worried about you, then Tate crawled off, and we didn't know where to look."

"I know, Freckles. But you don't need to worry about me."

"You were mad when you left. We thought you went to fight with Grandpa." She hugged him tight around the neck.

"I'm not that stupid. I just had to let off steam. You know your grandfather gets me mad with thinking he knows what's best for us. But I'll never sell. And I won't let him take you." He smoothed her hair and kissed her head. "That's a promise."

"Why did Carina get so upset about Tate?" Maddie leaned back, peering into his face.

"She lost a child. And I don't think she's over it."

"How?"

"I'm not sure, but she blames herself." He smoothed her hair. If anything happened to Maddie or Tate, he'd be beside himself with grief. He couldn't imagine what Carina had gone through.

"Do you think she'll ever marry you?" The arched eyebrow on his daughter's sweet face reminded him of Beth. She would want him to find someone to share his life with.

"I don't know. She's from the city. We know living out here takes some getting used to."

"But you'll ask her again?"

"We'll see." Brock stood, ending the conversation.

"If you didn't mean it the first time you shouldn't have asked." The censure in her young voice dropped him back down on the mattress.

"Why do you say that?" He stared at her, knowing she couldn't hide anything.

"Because you act like you really like her." She

shrugged her shoulders. "But act like a scared horse when you talk about marriage. Don't let Cindy and Mommy bother you."

The instincts of his daughter once again caught him unaware. "Why do you say that?"

"You haven't been interested in anyone since Cindy left. And you keep saying you don't need a woman." She grasped his hand, holding it between her two small palms. "But you like Carina, I can tell. And she likes you. She'd stay if you asked her."

Dread lay in his stomach like a rock. Did he want Carina to stay? He enjoyed the way she catered to him and the children, also having someone soft and willing in his arms. But would the novelty wear off for both of them? If so, he had to let her go before his children became hurt from the separation.

"I'll think about it. Go to sleep." He kissed her cheek and settled her back under the covers.

Descending the stairs, he thought about Maddie's words. Carina had become an important part of his children's lives. His heart picked up speed thinking of their night together and their almost tumbles in the hay. Her leaving wouldn't shatter his world—not really.

The smells wafting from the kitchen quickened his step. The sight quickened his heart. Carina leaned over the table placing food in the middle and straightening the place setting. Her hips rested against the top, while her round, firm bottom greeted his entrance.

Heat coursed to his loins as he stepped through the doorway. No woman had ever brought his body to the boiling point like the woman turning and smiling timidly. He crossed the room and pulled her into his arms while running his hands under her shirt. Her silky skin and curves aroused and satisfied.

"Don't," she said on a sharp intake of breath.

"Don't what?"

Her body stiffened under his caress. "Don't touch me like that."

The succinct words made him slowly slip his hands from under her shirt. When his palms met the cold air, he yearned to return them to her warmth. One glance at the blank expression and firm line of her lips told him to back off.

He'd done nothing since returning to be treated coldly. Incensed at himself for his boldness and her for allowing all that had transpired before, he refused to retreat. "What makes me unpleasant all of a sudden?"

"Not unpleasant. Never." Her gaze dropped toward the floor, she swallowed, and then looked back up at him. The determination in her blue eyes made his chest constrict. She was about to hit him with something.

"You have been without a woman for a long time. My being under your roof and vulnerable has led me to make bad decisions." She held up her hand when his mouth opened to speak. "I don't blame you. I've been a willing accomplice to our trysts. But I can't let my body rule my head, and I can't stay here any longer."

"Because of me? I can keep my hands to myself." He took a military stance, clasping his hands behind his back.

A weak smile wavered on her lips. "No. Not because you can't keep your hands to yourself. I lost your son tonight. I've grown fond of your children, and I can't stay here and wonder each day if I'll do something that will harm them." The tears and pain glistening in her eyes made it hard for him to keep his hands behind his back.

"You didn't put my children in danger. Tate is a boy. Boys do things that make you fearful, but you didn't do anything that would cause him harm." He couldn't stand back any longer. Stepping forward to gather her in his arms, she moved to the side, avoiding his embrace.

Carina wanted to feel his strong arms and believe his words, but she couldn't go through another day of fearing she'd put these children in jeopardy.

"Don't make this harder for all of us," she said, moving to the sink. "Sit down and eat. I'll leave in the morning."

Brock's warm breath against her neck made her gasp. The heat of his body pressed against her back sent tingles along every nerve. When he touched her, all sense of reason left her. This was what she'd hoped to avoid.

The deep voice seducing her whispered, "You would never intentionally hurt a child or any human being. You have no reason to feel guilty."

Fear gripped her. She turned, finding her nose pressed into the soft flannel of his shirt. Placing her hand on his firm chest, feeling the warmth of him under the worn material, she wanted to curl into his arms and savor the husky scent of him. But, she couldn't. She had to remain strong.

Pushing away, she said, "You know nothing about my baby."

"I know whatever happened wasn't your fault. And I don't believe you'd just run out on the kids like that. Not give them a chance to get used to the idea you're leaving." The frustration in his voice tugged at her conscience. He rubbed the back of his neck and stared into her eyes. Could he see the longing in her heart? She wanted to stay. But she couldn't until she came to grips with the guilt plaguing her.

"I'm not running out. I'm sparing them."

"That's not how they'll see it." He grasped her shoulders. Carina didn't want to argue with him. She'd had all she could take emotionally with the events of the evening. His touch was magnetic. She wanted to press her body against his and forget everything other than the feel of his hands and the taste of his kiss.

Gazing into his brown eyes, she dug deep to conjure the strength needed. "You don't know me as well as you think."

"I think I know you better than you know yourself." Brock slid his hands down her arm, spreading ripples of heat. "I say you sit here and tell me about losing your child while I eat."

Feared ricocheted in her belly. She relived that day every night when she shut her eyes. "I-I can't."

"You aren't leaving this house until I know what happened to make you think you caused your child's death." The anger in his words sent chills down her back.

She pulled the plate from the oven and set it on the table. "Good night." Tossing the hot pads on the table, she turned to leave. Brock grasped her arm firmly and pulled her onto his lap.

"Sorry. I'm not eating and you're not going to bed until I find out why you blame yourself." He circled her with both arms, holding her on his lap as his warm breath brushed across the top of her head.

"Why are you being so stubborn?" Tears slid down

her cheeks. No one had ever asked her about that day. Not her mother or Perry. Everyone had been sympathetic, but no one asked how she really felt about the incident.

"Because I want to see how you can blame yourself for something you had no control over." He hugged her and rested his chin on her head. "Start whenever you want. I don't mind sitting here all night holding you."

She wanted to snuggle against him and shut her eyes. However, she knew better than to let her defenses down around this man.

"What were you doing that day? Picking out baby stuff?" His non-committal question caught her off guard.

"I was helping Mom clean her shop and move furniture. We dusted and moved small pieces around to make it look like she had new inventory. Then I had an idea to set up a gorgeous old carved bed she had in the back of the store. It was close to the holidays, and she could fix it up like a scene from the *Night before Christmas*." Carina smiled, remembering how excited they both were over the idea.

"What happened after you rearranged the store?" His low, soft voice sounded like her own conscience urging her on.

"I went home. There was a message from Perry he wouldn't be home for dinner. A business meeting. He had meetings every night then. He was moving up. I heated a bowl of soup and sat down on the couch. I must have dozed off. I woke…" She swallowed and clutched her stomach. The pain she'd felt that night ripped through her just as violently.

"Shhh. You're okay." Brock put his hand on her

stomach and gently rubbed, releasing the tightness the memory brought on.

"I-I felt wet between my legs." She curled against Brock. "I called my mom, and she came to take me to the hospital."

"Where was your husband?" His censure cut through her painful recollection.

"No one could find him." The anger she'd felt that night at going through the brutal miscarriage alone struck her again. Her hands fisted as she clutched Brock's shirt.

"Is this the health problems you hinted at that first night on my porch?" His question threw her off.

"Y-yes."

"Why didn't you just tell me? None of this is your fault. It was an accident."

"No, if I hadn't insisted on moving that heavy bed, I'd have a child to hold in my arms and love." She pushed at him. Didn't he see? It was her fault. She knew better than to strain in the last stages of pregnancy. She'd read all the books.

Brock took her head in his hands and looked into her eyes. "You had nothing to do with what happened. Fate took that child from you. There was nothing you could have done differently." He hugged her. "I know if something happened to Maddie or Tate, I'd be beside myself with grief. I understand the grief, but not the blame." He held her away from him. Conviction shone in his eyes. "You would never hurt anyone. Don't hurt yourself."

"I didn't even get to hold her." Carina broke into sobs of grief.

No one had let her hold her baby.

Twenty

Carina stretched. That was the best night's sleep she'd had in over a year. She rubbed her eyes. It felt like the Sahara Desert moved under her eyelids. Her throat was raw. She ran her hands over her puffy face. Physically, she was a wreck, but emotionally, she felt better. Finally, someone had allowed her to grieve.

But what must Brock think of her this morning? She dressed quickly and headed to the kitchen.

The man in her thoughts stood at the sink filling the coffee pot. "Morning," she said, moving past him to grab the skillet.

"You still plan to leave today?" His quiet question shook her.

"If you think it's—" Before the words were out, his arms embraced her and his lips seduced hers. The skillet fell to the floor with a thud when her arms wrapped around his neck. He lifted her off the ground, kissing her neck. She leaned back, allowing him all he wished.

"Sheesh!" Maddie's voice invaded the humming in

Carina's head.

Carina unhooked her arms, and Brock slid her down the front of him until her feet landed on the floor.

"It's not nice to sneak up on people," Brock said, tucking Carina against his side.

"Not like you two weren't making too much noise to hear me." Maddie picked up the skillet and placed it on the stove.

Carina's face heated. What must the girl think of them? Of her?

"You're right Maddie, we shouldn't be acting like that." Carina stepped away from Brock. He gathered her back beside him.

"You need to get used to this," Brock said, grinning like he'd just won the lottery. "We worked things out last night."

Carina's heart pattered as her stomach took a dive. What had they worked out? She turned to Brock with her hands on her hips. "We did?"

Maddie jumped up and down. "You asked her to marry you!"

Carina backed up, holding her hands out in front of her. "We didn't talk about any such thing." She narrowed her eyes. "Why are you saying this? Are you trying to make me feel worse if I decide to leave?"

"You can't leave!" Maddie exclaimed, throwing her arms around Carina.

Her stomach did another flip, Carina glared at Brock. What was he trying to do?

She continued to stare daggers at Brock as the phone on the wall trilled. He growled and moved across the room, snatching the receiver from the instrument.

"Hello." His voice was gruff, but his eyebrows

arched up, and he shot a glance her way. "Yes, she's here. Just a minute." He held his hand over the mouthpiece. "There's a guy on the phone. He says it's urgent he talks to you."

Carina shook her head. She couldn't think of any man that would call her here. Her employer at the nanny agency was female. Besides that woman, her mother and Georgie were the only people with this phone number.

Shrugging she moved across the room to take the phone. She held the phone to her ear and felt her guts squeeze, she knew that background noise.

"How did you get this number?" She wasn't about to be cordial to a man who took away nearly everything in the divorce.

"Easy, honey."

"I'm not your honey. I asked you how you got this number?"

"From your mom. You know she and I still talk." His condescending attitude had her grinding her teeth.

"Bully for you." In her peripheral vision, Brock sent Maddie out of the room. But he poured himself a cup of coffee and sat down at the table. She glared at him and turned her back.

"Hey, you're the one who left."

"Because you were boffing the CEO's ugly daughter when I needed you." She heard Brock snort. Why wasn't he giving her any privacy?

"You just used that as an excuse. We know why you wanted a divorce. Because you couldn't tell me—"

"Why did you call?" Carina's hand ached from squeezing the phone. He'd badgered her after the miscarriage, saying she should have done this or that, when it all came down to he wasn't there when she needed him, and he wasn't big enough to admit it.

"That certificate of deposit we have jointly?"

"Yeah?" She didn't like where this was going.

"I need you to sign off so I can use that as collateral against a deal that will double—"

"No! We agreed to keep it until the maturity date. If it comes out sooner, we get penalized. I worked hard for my share that is in there and I'm not going to let you lose it." He hadn't changed a bit. Always trying to double his money on "get rich quick" schemes. And always losing her money.

"Honey, it's a sure thing. I can double your half, too."

"No! You can't touch it without my signature, and I'm not going to sign." She heard Brock get up and walk to the sink. Was he finally going to leave?

"I'll get that money out with or without your signature. I thought you'd be willing to help me out but I see you're just a bitter woman." The phone thunked in her ear and went silent.

"Damn!" She slammed the phone down and whirled around. Brock had his head in the refrigerator.

"I have to leave," she said, still trying to figure out how Perry could get the money without her signature. Unless… she wouldn't put it past him to have someone pretend to be her to get the money. When it came to money, he would stop at nothing to gamble it on a risky venture.

"Just like that?" Brock turned to her, a carton of eggs in his hand. "You get off the phone and say, I have to leave." He put the carton down so hard, that she winced hoping the eggs didn't break. "I thought you were going to give this more time?"

"I'll come back. I have to make sure Perry doesn't take my money from the one joint account we have left." She had to make him see she wasn't leaving because of him or the kids.

"Sure you will. You'll get back there in the city and decide that life's better than what we can give you here. I've seen it before." He stomped out of the kitchen.

Carina followed him into the mudroom. She grabbed his arm and pulled, trying to make him look at her.

"I have to do this."

"Why? Is money more important than this family?"

Jamming her fists on her hips she glared at him. "When hasn't money motivated everything you do for this family? And for your information, that money is my retirement fund. I don't plan to live my whole life working like you'll be on this ranch."

The tick in his jaw and the way he crammed his hat on his head, she knew she'd spoken out of line. Before she could retract the words, he was out the door.

"Brock! Come back. I didn't..." The truck roared to life and revved down the road.

He thought she was using the money as an excuse to leave. Especially after last night, but she wasn't. That money was her retirement. And she'd be damned if she was going to let Perry lose it.

Carina spotted Maddie running to the barn from the kitchen window. The girl had tennis shoes, a sweatshirt, and nothing on her head. What was wrong with these people? You can't go running around in this weather half-dressed.

Tate wailed in the living room. She'd layer Tate and herself up to take a coat out to Maddie. Why the girl would do such a thing was beyond her. She was the one who taught Carina how to dress for this climate.

When they were both bundled up in hats, scarves, warm coats and boots, Carina headed to the barn. The sound of running hooves echoed in the snowy air. She glanced toward the hill behind the barn and saw Maddie and Cookie hurrying in the opposite direction Brock had gone.

"Maddie! Come Back! Maddie!" The horse and rider continued over the rise. "I have to stop her." Carina studied the squirming boy in her arms. She couldn't drive the sports car across the country Maddie and the horse were traversing. She'd have to take a horse.

She couldn't take Tate with her on the horse. But she couldn't leave him home alone. *Willie T.* She'd call Willie T. But it would take him too long to get there and Maddie's tracks could be filled in with the snow that powdered Tate's hat and shoulders.

Her feet shifted in the snow as indecision weighed on her heart. She had to go after Maddie. Who knew what could happen to her, not to mention, she could get hypothermia the way she was dressed.

But that would mean leaving Tate home alone. She couldn't risk taking him with her on a horse. Not when she was so inexperienced. But leaving him home alone? Her heart thudded in her chest. She couldn't risk either of them.

Think Carina, Think! She chewed on her bottom lip and knew she wasted valuable time. Making the decision, she headed to the house. In the living room, she pulled Tate's playpen to the middle of the room where he couldn't grab anything. She placed several of his safest toys in the pen and turned on the radio.

She scribbled a quick note and grabbed Maddie's warmest coat. At the barn, she caught the easiest horse and saddled it as fast as her inexperienced hands could. She heaved on the cinch strap, hoping the cinch pulled tight enough. Brock had always checked this and usually tightened it more before she got on.

The back of her mind cursed her for leaving Tate alone. But he was warm and in his playpen, nothing could happen to him, unlike his sister racing through the snowstorm in nothing but a sweatshirt and tennis shoes.

Carina tied Maddie's coat to the leather strings on the back of the saddle and led the horse out of the barn. She could barely make out Cookie's tracks in the snow. Mounting, she kneed the horse into a bumpy trot. Peering over the horse's shoulder, she followed the vanishing tracks over the hill and out of sight of the house and Tate.

Twenty-one

Brock drove only a couple miles down the county road before turning around and heading back to the house. The more he thought about it, the more he realized, he should have heard Carina out. He'd made his assumptions based on two other women. And so far, Carina had proven to be completely different from both of them.

At the house, he stomped the snow from his boots and entered the backdoor expecting to be mauled by Maddie. "Maddie? Carina?" he called, hanging up his coat and hat. A country western song drifted down the hall from the living room. Brock peeked his head around the kitchen door. No one. Tate let out a happy shriek. Brock smiled and hurried to the living room. His son sat in the playpen, dressed in his coat, his hat on the playpen floor, and happily spinning a ball on the toy in the corner of his pen.

"Where is everyone, Tater? And why are you in your coat" Brock picked up his son and scanned the room. Where were Carina and Maddie?

He carried Tate into the kitchen. Propped in the middle of the table he found a note.

Maddie took off without a coat. I went after her. Carina.

Took off? Where? And when? The back of his neck tensed, and a slight pain throbbed behind his eyes. Where were they and how long ago did they leave? He walked back into the living room, plucked Tate's hat from the playpen, and pulled the boy's mittens on. After Tate was bundled up, Brock pulled on dry boots, coat, and gloves.

"C'mon, we need to find your sister and Carina." Brock scooped Tate up in one arm and headed to the corrals. "Damn!" Two horses were missing. His heart lodged in his throat. *Not again.* He wouldn't lose someone he loved to another horse accident.

Running to the front of the barn, he studied the snow. He barely made out round indentions far enough apart to be horse prints.

Brock ran to the pickup. He strapped Tate into the car seat, started the vehicle, and groped under the seat to reassure himself the first aid kit was still there. Slamming the pickup into gear, he headed out following the tracks. Each gulley he came to brought bile up his throat. It was a gulley where he found Beth near death. She'd lain there so long there had been nothing anyone could do. *Nothing he could do.* She'd gone on a ride like any other day. When he'd returned from fixing fence with Maddie, he'd gone looking for her. And found his wife *beyond* help. He'd known from his stint in the Gulf, she wasn't going to make it. When Johnson turned his accusing eyes on Brock, he'd let the man make him think it was his fault. When in reality, just like Carina's miscarriage, it was fate.

Fate wasn't going to take away someone he loved again.

Riding horses in these conditions, he should catch up to them in no time. He pushed the pickup through two-foot snow drifts following the trail of the two females he held in his heart

***

Carina's face and fingers felt like she'd slept on a pillow full of needles. She didn't want to think how cold Maddie must be with as little clothing as the child wore when she left. Carina worried that leaving Tate hadn't been the right thing to do. How could she have left a child so young alone? *Please don't let my negligence harm another child.*

Topping the rise, she spotted a riderless horse. Fear spiraled in her belly. She urged her horse faster, but the animal breathed hard, and she could feel its body quiver from fatigue. Just when she spotted a body in the snow, her horse stumbled, and she flew through the air. Her leg caught in the stirrup and something snapped. She landed in the snow and everything went black.

***

Brock shot over a rise. His headlights caught the shape of two riderless horses through the flurry of snowflakes. *"No!"* he screamed, sliding the pickup sideways. He checked to make sure Tate was secure and jumped out of the vehicle, scanning the area beyond the horses. He spotted Carina. Running to her, he dropped to his knees. "No, not again." His stomach twisted with dread. He reached out to stroke her wind-burned cheek.

Her eyes fluttered open, and he gently rested her

head on his leg. Relief whooshed out of him like a tire without a valve stem.

"No, forget me. Maddie," Carina whispered. "Find Maddie, she doesn't have a coat."

"I'll put you in the pickup first." Brock started to scoop her into his arms.

"No! Leave me, find Maddie!" she said vehemently. "She needs you."

Carina's leg lay at an odd angle, but if that was her only injury, she was right; Maddie would be freezing if she sprawled in the snow.

"I'll be back as soon as I find Maddie."

Carina gave him a weak smile and closed her eyes. The pale skin and grimace revealed her pain.

He gently placed her hooded head on the snow and scanned the white vastness. The snow had been disrupted in a spot twenty-five yards away. He plodded through the knee-high snow and found a small, dark lump partially covered in snow.

"Maddie? Maddie, it's Dad." She wore only jeans and a sweatshirt. Why had she ridden out in so few clothes? She knew better than that. "Why?" he asked as he slowly assessed her body for injuries. Again, he used his military training. He didn't want to think about the last instance. This time would have a different ending. It must or he wouldn't be able to live.

He evaluated the situation and didn't find any bones broken. Brock scooped Maddie's limp body into his arms and carried her back to the pickup. He noticed on his way by, Carina had sat up against a snow bank. That was a good sign.

Tate let out a squeal when Brock set Maddie on the pickup seat and covered her with a blanket. The sound didn't cause her cold body to show any indication of hearing the screech. Brock twisted the knob on the heater to high and closed the door, heading back for Carina.

"I think it's just my leg," she said when he knelt beside her. "Maddie?"

"She's unconscious. Don't know if it's from a blow to the head or cold." He slid his arm under Carina's legs and scooped her up into his arms. His heart fluttered with happiness. She only had minor injuries, now to get Maddie home and assess her injuries and get to the bottom of her reckless ride.

"I-is Tate okay? I didn't want to leave him alone, but I knew I couldn't bring him out in this." The worry on her face and in her voice showed her love for the child.

Brock kissed her. "He's fine. You were brave and stupid to head out in this" He pulled the door open and set her on the seat. She winced when her leg had to be turned to get it in the cab.

He fussed to make her comfortable.

"Forget about me. Get us home so we can take care of Maddie." Carina pushed him away and closed the door. He saw her face scrunch at the pain of twisting her injured leg.

Brock hurried to the driver's side and climbed in. He turned the pickup around to find the horses standing in their way.

"Oh! What about the horses?" Carina asked, watching them huddle together.

"If I can catch them, I'll throw the tack in the back and they can survive until we get them rounded up again." He put the vehicle in neutral and went back out into the cold. His luck held. Neither horse appeared spooked and stood while Brock removed their saddles and bridles. Once they were free of the tack, the animals took off in the direction of the ranch house.

"They'll probably beat us home," Brock said, sliding back in the driver's seat and following the horses. He tried to go fast, yet, not jar Carina or Maddie too much. Before long the house came into sight. He looked over at Carina. Her hand rested on Maddie's cheek.

"She'll be fine. She's young and resilient," he said to reassure her and himself.

"I don't understand why she took off like that." Carina looked at him. "She always scolded me for not dressing warm enough."

Brock shook his head. "I'm not sure either. We'll have to wait until she comes around to ask."

He drove the pickup onto the yard, close to the back door. Carina started to open the door. He leaned across, taking her hand, "I'm going to put Tate in his playpen and come back for Maddie. Then I'll get you." He squeezed her hand. "Don't move." She nodded and dropped her hand in her lap.

Tate squirmed all the way into the house. Brock plopped him into his playpen with all his warm clothes on. They could worry about unbundling him later. He returned for Maddie. Cradling his daughter in his arms, he swore as a familiar vehicle pulled up the drive. Brock hurried into the house and propped Maddie up on the couch, tucking all the afghans and blankets he could find in close proximity around her motionless body.

He stepped out the back door and was confronted by Johnson.

"What the hell are you doing to my granddaughter?" the old man bellowed and tried to push Brock to the side.

The accusation in the man's voice set Brock's anger up a notch. "If you don't get out of my way, I can't do anything to help her." He pushed the man aside as Carina opened the pickup door.

"I told you to stay." Brock hurried to her side.

"I only opened the door. My hand isn't broke." Carina nodded her head toward the man entering the house. "And I don't want you two arguing right now. It won't help Maddie." She slid an arm around his neck, and he picked her up. She didn't weigh any more than Maddie.

Brock wanted to charge into the living room and demand the cancerous man leave, but he had to take care of the woman he loved—the thought hit him in the gut. Yes, loved. He'd realized it when he feared the worst for her and Maddie. Forgetting his father-in-law and concentrating on the woman, Brock took a seat on the bench and held Carina on his lap as he unlaced his boots. Kicking off the wet footwear, his cold feet started to tingle. He sat a moment enjoying the feel of the woman he held. She'd pushed the hood of the coat off her head and the dark strands of hair danced with electricity.

He kissed her firmly on the lips. She melted into his embrace. This was something he wanted from now until he died.

"Quit diddling with that woman and get in here and look after your daughter," called their unwanted visitor.

Brock started to voice his retort, but Carina placed a hand over his mouth. "Think of Maddie."

He unzipped her coat and pulled her arms out. "As soon as I get you settled on the couch next to Maddie, I'm sending that thorn in my side packing then calling Willie T." He dropped Carina's coat next to his boots and stood in one motion, hugging her to his chest as he carried her to the couch.

"Her color looks better," Carina said when Brock settled her on the couch, being careful of her broken leg. If he wasn't remaining so calm, she would have panicked by now. Where was this man when she needed someone a year ago? Why couldn't Perry have been this cool? Maybe then she would have realized the miscarriage wasn't her fault. *If her husband had helped her see the truth, rather than blame her.*

She cringed when Brock slammed his fisted hands on his hips and turned to Mr. Johnson.

"I'm only going to ask you once. Please leave. I have to check my daughter for injuries—"

"You haven't checked her yet? Damn, boy you're just as irresponsible as when your wife died." The older man's face reddened.

"If I didn't have to deal with you, I'd be checking her!" Brock snapped.

"Brock." Carina started to stand.

He rushed to her side.

"Don't move. You're only making the break worse." He gently swung her legs back on the couch.

"Mr. Johnson, I'm sure you are just as concerned about your granddaughter as Brock. But if you keep antagonizing him, he can't do what needs done." Carina grimaced at the pain shooting up her leg. On a whoosh of air, she added. "Please sit and be quiet if you truly care about Maddie." The man glared at her and plopped on a chair, crossing his arms over his ample paunch. She waved a weak hand at Brock, "Go call Willie T."

"I'll be right back. And when I get Maddie checked and comfortable, we'll set that leg." The smile he gave her was forced. She'd had a first aid class in her day and knew setting her leg would be painful.

Leaning over, she grabbed the playpen and pulled it toward her. The old wood floors made it easier to slide than if it sat on carpet. She could have asked the man sitting in the chair glaring at her to help, but she wasn't sure he would sit back down once he helped.

"Come on, Tate. Let me take your boots and coat off." She put her hands under his arms to lift him out and realized she couldn't do it from her position on the couch. Shifting only made her leg hurt so bad she couldn't concentrate. Carina glanced at Mr. Johnson. He'd tipped his head back, his eyes closed. The pain on his face wasn't from a physical injury. Was he replaying the day his daughter was found?

"Guess we'll just get the coat and hat off right now," she said, unbundling the boy. Glancing at Maddie, she thought the girl's eyelashes fluttered.

Brock returned with torn sheets and short lengths of wood. "Willie T's on his way. I need to check for any bruising. Rushing out like she did with no coat and then falling in the snow, we need to keep her warm and watch for possible exposure."

Mr. Johnson sat forward hanging on every word and looking as though he wanted to say something. Carina was surprised when he just pressed his lips tighter.

"Check Maddie first," Carina said, pulling her injured leg away from Brock when he knelt in front of her.

He smiled. "You're one stubborn woman when it comes to the kids."

"Mine is only a minor injury. It's Maddie I'm concerned about." For all Brock's smiles and flippancy, the creases in his forehead and pain in his eyes proved he worried just as much.

"Do as the woman says and check my granddaughter."

Brock ignored the man, but Carina flashed him a warning look and returned her attention to Brock.

He tenderly untucked the blanket around his daughter and raised her shirt. Carina boosted her body higher with her hands to catch sight of the child's body. No abnormal coloring appeared on her chest or stomach. He rolled her to her side and checked her back. Nothing there either.

"Check her head for lumps," Carina suggested. The only reason she broke her leg from the fall was her shoe catching in the stirrup. Other than that, falling into the snow had actually been soft and cushy. However, if Maddie happened to find a rock with her head… Carina didn't want to think about that. Positive thoughts. That's what she had to send to Maddie.

Brock sent Carina what he hoped was an encouraging smile and ignored the man watching his every move as he gently ran his hands through Maddie's hair feeling for bumps or cuts. He wrapped her back up in the blanket. All they could do was keep her warm and wait and see. And call the doc if she didn't come around in an hour or so.

"Let's take care of that leg." He knelt in front of Carina.

"What about Maddie?" Johnson sprang out of the chair and headed across the room.

"There doesn't appear to be any breaks or surface injuries. All we can do is wait for her to come around." Brock dismissed the man, turning back to Carina.

"You think I believe what you have to say?" The man grabbed Brock's shoulder, spinning him around. "You killed my daughter and you think I'll stand here and watch you kill her daughter?"

Anger and frustration churned in Brock's cut. He swatted the man's hand off his shoulder. "I did not kill your daughter! I loved her and did everything I knew to try and keep her alive—just like I'm doing now." Brock wanted to land a fist in the man's protruding gut, but that wouldn't help Carina or Maddie. "Sit down Maxwell or leave. Those are your only choices." Brock turned back to Carina. Her pale face made him drop to his knees. She was in more pain than she let on.

"Do you know how to set a leg?" Even though Carina questioned him, she didn't pull her leg away when Brock unlaced her athletic shoe.

"I was in the military, remember? I had extensive medical training there and I keep up my Red Cross card. Living isolated like this, it's a necessity." He gently slid the shoe off. "It wasn't very smart riding in these shoes."

"I know. It's the reason my leg broke. This foot didn't slide out of the stirrup when the horse went down." She grimaced as he sawed at the denim of her pants with his pocket knife. "You could go in the kitchen and get some scissors," she offered between gritting her teeth.

Brock's face heated with embarrassment. He

usually worked on cows. They didn't complain about his rough treatment. "Yeah, guess I should." He threw a glance toward Johnson as he exited the room. The man looked older, less threatening.

Brock found the scissors and headed back to the living room as Willie T stomped in through the back door.

"Where's my girl?" he asked, tossing his coat and scarf on the pile by the bench.

"In here. She still hasn't come around, but her color is getting better." Brock motioned to the couch and went back to exposing Carina's injured leg.

"Hello Maxwell," Willie T said. Brock glanced up in time to see the two men's gazes clash. He knew Willie T wouldn't do anything, but with Johnson, you never knew.

"Willie T." Johnson remained seated his mouth once again set in a disapproving straight line.

Brock shrugged the man off. He had to get Carina's leg set. Once the fabric was removed, he could see the end of the bone bulging under her skin.

He ran a hand over the knot forming at the base of his skull. This was someone he loved. He didn't want to cause her pain, but knew he had to set the bone and get it immobilized.

Willie T looked down at the leg and whistled before saying, "I'll get her some whiskey."

Brock took Carina's hand. "You're lucky that end hasn't popped out." As soon as the words escaped, he realized he'd said too much. Her eyes rolled back, and her skin went white before she sunk back against the couch.

"How'd you knock her out?" Willie T asked,

returning with a cup and flask of whiskey.

"I opened my big mouth." Brock motioned to Willie T. "Might as well do this before she regains consciousness. Help me put her on the floor." When Carina was flat on the floor, he looked at her pale face.

"You have to do this," Willie T said, putting a hand on his shoulder. The touch gave him a feeling of peace and knowledge that he knew what to do.

"You hold her leg at the knee."

With Willie T's help, they managed to get the leg back in place. Brock wrapped the leg and had the sticks attached to either side of her leg when Carina stirred.

"I think it hurts worse," she muttered, blinking back tears.

"There will be swelling and trauma in the area of the break, from the bone tearing at everything." Brock placed his hands under her arms and gently placed her back on the end of the couch. Willie T brought over a footrest and they propped her injured leg up with pillows.

"Here, drink this," Willie T said, holding a glass of whiskey.

"No thanks. Bring me some ibuprofen. Alcohol and I don't mix well. With a broken leg, I can't be running for a place to vomit." The tight grin she flashed Willie T had Brock hurrying to the medicine cabinet for the pills.

"I'll take some," Johnson said, reaching for the bottle.

When Carina was settled comfortably, Brock picked up Tate and motioned for Willie T to follow him into the kitchen.

"I'm worried about Maddie. She should have come

around by now." Brock kept his voice low, so it wouldn't carry to Carina. He'd kept a nonchalant attitude about Maddie's condition around Carina, but he didn't like the fact Maddie hadn't woken up yet. It was becoming too much like her mother. "I also don't like Johnson watching me like a vulture."

"I think he's getting his eyes opened. Do not worry about the man." Willie T placed a hand on his shoulder and squeezed. "Maddie is young, she will be fine. Why was she riding in the storm without proper clothing?"

"I don't know. Carina said, she just looked out and saw Maddie taking off on Cookie without a coat. It worried her, so she put Tate in the playpen, left me a note, and headed out after her." Brock massaged the back of his neck. "It was a good thing she did. Her tracks were nearly filled in with snow when I started after them." He looked at the man standing in front of him. "If I'd tried to find only Maddie's prints, I may never have found her."

"Carina is a smart woman. She did what was right." Willie T moved to the stove and felt the coffee pot. He grunted and pulled it off the burner, heading for the sink.

"We should try and get some broth or something down both of them, don't you think?" Brock dug in the cupboard for a can of soup.

"Yeah." Willie T put the pot back on the stove and lit the fire under it. "I think I'll go sit with them while you make that soup."

Brock nodded his head. He needed some time alone to think about what he could have lost today. His daughter and the woman he loved.

Twenty-two

Carina felt someone watching her. She slowly opened her eyes and saw Maddie's eyelashes flutter shut. The child was faking. Of that Carina was certain. Did Mr. Johnson see Maddie's eyes open? She glanced at the man. He had his head tipped back and his eyes closed.

Willie T came back into the room. "That was some scare you two gave Brock," he said, sitting on the chair next to Carina.

Carina motioned to Willie T to watch Maddie. "Yeah, I don't know why Maddie took off like she did. She's too smart to go riding off without a coat." Carina pulled the quilt up under her chin. "I'm still frozen."

The shrill peal of the phone echoed through the house. Willie T and Carina smiled when Maddie jumped at the sound.

Carina heard the deep tone of Brock's voice as he talked. His steps thumped down the hall, and he grabbed the phone on a side table, stretching the cord to make it reach Carina.

"It's your mom," he said, putting Tate in the playpen and moving to touch Maddie's face.

"Mom, thanks for calling," Carina said, trying to decide how much to tell her about the day's happenings.

"Dear, I had to call. I just got off the phone with Perry. He wants me to come down and sign something…"

"That sneaky, conniving… Mom, don't sign anything. I'll be there as soon as I can get a cast on this leg." Carina shifted and pain shot up her leg.

"Cast! Leg! What on earth is going on there?" Her mother's voice spiraled up an octave, meaning she was moving into panic mode.

"I'm fine. Brock and Willie T have it stabilized. We're waiting for Maddie to wake up so we can go to the hospital and get my leg tended by a physician."

"How did it happen? My word darling no wonder Perry was so worried about you."

"Mom, he isn't worried about me. He is worried about getting my money so he can spend it on some scam." Carina took a deep breath. "He must have found out I have your name as the second on it. Do not sign it. I don't want him to lose that money. It's the money from Dad's trust."

Her mother gasped on the other end of the phone. "Why does he want that? It's yours. It wasn't even part of the divorce."

"Exactly, he's trying to get his hands on it for some reason. He said to invest and make me rich, but I think he got himself in deep and is using it to bail him out. Don't sign anything. I'm coming as soon as I can and will make sure he can never touch it."

"Okay, Sweetheart. I'm glad I called you first."

"I am, too, Mom. Don't worry. I'll call you as soon as I know when I can get back." Carina replaced the phone and looked up. Willie T and Brock watched her intently as well as a wide-awake Maddie.

"Don't leave us!" Maddie cried, sitting up and throwing her arms around Carina.

"Maddie!" Relief softened Johnson's tone as he crossed the room with his arms outstretched.

"Why are you here?" Maddie's fearful eyes glanced from her father's surprised face to her grandfather as she clung to Carina.

"It was lucky I happened by when your father brought you home. Come on, I'll take you to the hospital where you can get a real looking over from a doctor." Johnson reached for the girl.

"No!" Maddie clung tighter to Carina. "I don't want to go with you and I *don't* want Carina to leave."

"I'm not leaving you." Carina smoothed the hair out of Maddie's face. "I just have to go back to Chicago and make sure my ex-husband can't get his hands on the trust my father left to me. It's money I plan to use for my future." She held the child close. Happiness hummed through her. They'd come so close to losing her.

She put space between them. "Why did you take off like you did?"

Maddie bit her lip and looked down.

Carina raised her chin and made her gaze into her eyes. "Maddie, what made you take off on Cookie without proper clothing? And in the middle of a snowstorm."

"I heard you on the phone, saying you were going

to leave." Tears trickled down her cheeks. "I was mad you would just leave like that. Without even thinking about us being left alone."

"Oh, Maddie! I'm coming back. I just have to take care of this money matter, and I'll be back. I promise."

Brock scooted across the couch, sandwiching Maddie in between himself and Carina. "How about we all come to Chicago with you, meet your mother, and have a small wedding?"

Mr. Johnson jammed his hands on his hips and glared at them. "I've never heard of anything so ludicrous."

"Really! You and Carina are getting married!" Maddie put an arm around Brock's neck and one around Carina's neck.

"You can't marry the nanny. She's nothing—"

Brock silenced Mr. Johnson with a scowl. "She's everything this family needs and more."

Carina stared into Brock's eyes and saw he meant every word. Her heart thrummed in her chest.

"That way, you have to come back with us," he said, pushing a strand of hair behind her ear.

"I-I don't know what to say." She knew he was serious but she hadn't heard the words to make her say yes. She glanced into Maddie's pleading eyes and squeezed her eyes shut. This family needed her. And she needed this family. But she couldn't afford to have her heart broken. She now realized she wasn't really in love with Perry. She'd been blinded by his façade and now saw the real man.

She studied Brock. This man she loved. Completely. But she didn't want a one-sided relationship. And she wasn't willing to tell him, knowing he wasn't bound to reciprocate those same feelings.

As if knowing her turmoil, Willie T snatched Maddie from between them. "Come on Maxwell, there's coffee brewing in the kitchen." The astute man headed down the hall to the kitchen carrying Maddie and leading Mr. Johnson.

Carina wished he hadn't taken the child. With Maddie in between them, she could keep her mind focused on the question and not the attraction she felt for the man.

Brock wrapped his arms around her, being careful not to put any strain on her leg, and drew her onto his lap.

"I'm not asking you to marry me for my kids." He kissed her temple. The chaste kiss sent tendrils of desire whispering through her body. "I'm asking you to be my wife because I've fallen in love with you."

Her heart raced. *He loved her*. She put her arms around his neck. "Really? You love me?"

"Woman, I've loved you just about since you first set foot in the door. Your kind, compassionate, love my children, and respect my way of life. What isn't there to love about you?"

"My past." She couldn't look at him.

"What about your past?" he splayed his fingers through her hair and held her face in front of his.

"I-I may not be able to have any more children. And I know how good you are with Maddie and Tate."

He drew her face up to his and kissed her, slow and deliberate. When he released her, she couldn't think.

"Carina, if we have children together wonderful, if we don't, I'll not stop loving you."

Tears of joy slipped from the corners of her eyes. "That's all I need to hear. Yes, I'll marry you. Any time and any place."

Epilogue

"What do you think of your new sister?" Carina asked, holding three-day-old Beth for her big sister and brother to see.

"She's adorable," Maddie said, in breathless wonder, while Tate poked at her with his pudgy finger.

Carina gazed into the eyes of the proud father. She still couldn't believe she made it all the way through the pregnancy and produced a beautiful, little girl.

"You did good, Mommy," Brock said, placing a kiss on her forehead.

"Yeah, she's just as sweet as her namesake," Mr. Johnson chimed in.

Carina smiled up at the man. After having witnessed Brock's care of her and his granddaughter, the man had finally forgiven Brock for Beth's death. His realization that Brock had nothing to do with the fate of his beloved daughter had brought the estranged family together. Giving Maddie and Tate a grandfather.

It still surprised Carina that the beautiful child in her arms had been conceived on their postponed honeymoon. One they took after the sale of the cattle. The profits had surpassed Brock's expectations, paying off the past debts and allowing them a belated honeymoon trip to the Oregon Coast.

Tate patted his new sister. "Sissy."

"You have to be gentle with her," Maddie admonished.

"Mommy, too," Brock added, taking her hand.

Tate patted Carina's knee. "Gentle."

Her love for every family member was overwhelming. Batting her eyes to keep the tears of happiness from spilling, she said, "I couldn't have made it through this without all of your love."

***

Contemporary Western Romance
Perfectly Good Nanny
Bridled Heart
Catch the Rain

Tumbling Creek Ranch Novella Series
8 Seconds to Love
Love Me Anyway
The Wrong Cowboy to Love
Collateral Love

Historical Western Romance
For A Sister's Love
Gambling on an Angel
Improper Pinkerton

Halsey Brothers Series
Marshal in Petticoats
Outlaw in Petticoats
Miner in Petticoats
Doctor in Petticoats
Logger in Petticoats

Halsey Homecoming Series
Laying Claim
Staking Claim
Claiming a Heart
A Husband for Christmas

Letters of Fate
Davis
Isaac

Brody

Silver Dollar Saloon
Savannah
Lottie
Freedom

Native American Spirit Trilogy
Spirit of the Mountain
Spirit of the Lake
Spirit of the Sky

About the Author

Paty Jager is an award-winning author of 50+ novels, 8 novellas, and numerous anthologies of murder mystery and western romance. All her work has Western or Native American elements in them along with hints of humor and engaging characters. Paty and her husband raise alfalfa hay in rural eastern Oregon. Riding horses and battling rattlesnakes, she not only writes the western lifestyle, she lives it.

Check out her website to see all of the historical and contemporary western books she's written as well as your mystery series. https://www.patyjager.net

If You'd like to learn more about Paty and the books she writes you can follow her on her author Facebook page or join her newsletter.

Website: https://www.patyjager.net
Blog: https://writingintothesunset.net/
Newsletter: https://bit.ly/2IhmWcm
Facebook – Author Paty Jager

If you enjoyed this or any of Paty's books, please leave a review on a site selling her books. Thank you!

Thank you for purchasing this Windtree Press
publication. For other books of the heart, please visit
our website at www.windtreepress.com.

For questions or more information contact us
at info@windtreepress.com.

Windtree Press
Corvallis, OR